A Young-Adult Novel

VIRGINIA M. SCOTT

Publishing Partners

BOOKS BY VIRGINIA M. SCOTT

Belonging

Palace of the Princess

Balancing Act

Finding Abby

The Carnelian Door

Don't Cross Your Heart, Katie Krieg

Publishing Partners
Port Townsend, WA 98368
www.publishing-partners.com

LCCN: 2017938676
ISBN: 978-1-944887-21-6
eISBN: 978-1-944887-23-0

Cover Design: Marcia Breece
Book Design: Marcia Breece

Dedication

For Amy

"What's this?" my friend Rachel asked as she riffled through my notebook after school. Her question sort of started it all.

"Did you find the assignment sheet?" I was ninety-nine percent sure that Mr. Breen's assignment on constitutional amendments was due on Monday, but Rachel thought he'd meant tomorrow. The sheet would settle it. Across my room, I pulled an old sweatshirt over my head.

"Katie, would you come over here?"

"Sure. What's the rush?"

"This." she said as she held out a typewriter-sized sheet of paper by one corner. It might have been smelly laundry from her look.

"Ick. Due tomorrow?" I walked closer. She just kept staring at the paper with this really spacey look. "Rachel?"

"Here. You'd better look at this. I didn't mean to read it, but the words jumped right out at me."

Words?

"That's okay," I assured her.

Then I looked at the "words" and did a double take.

"What is this? It looks like somebody hacked letters out of a magazine and pasted them on," I said in amazement. They were crooked, different-sized alphabet letters, and the page was sort of puckered from the glue holding them on.

"Yeah, that's why I was staring. It's ... I don't know ... creepy."

"You can say that again."

It got a whole lot creepier when I read the message:

i KNOW you'Re HaviNG

a THiNG WiTH GRaySON

"What!" I exploded. Then I felt a dizzying rush as the blood drained from my head. Was I going to pass out?

"Katie? Katie, are you all right?"

"All right? No, I'm not all right. Rachel, this is terrible. Grayson? Grayson as in Mr. Timothy Grayson?"

"Do you know any other Graysons?"

"No."

"Then it must be him."

I looked at her in astonishment. "But he's our teacher. This is so embarrassing. I mean, a 'thing' with him. Does that mean what I think it does?"

"Yeah, I'd say so."

Mr. Grayson's blond, twenty-something image flitted through my mind, and I could feel my face growing hot. A thing?

"I just can't believe this," I said. I crushed the paper and tossed it into the wastebasket. "It's total garbage."

"I know. Hey, maybe you got the note by mistake."

"Yeah, that must be it." But the moment of feeling

better burst like a bubble.

"What if I didn't?"

"One way or another, it's just a stupid prank."

"Not a very funny one." Then a horrible thought seized me. "What'll I do if people hear about this?"

"I don't know why they should, not if we don't tell anybody."

"Promise you won't."

"All right, but I wonder if Grayson ought to know that trash like this is being circulated."

"Are you kidding? Tell him? Rachel, I'd die. Grayson and me? I don't know whether to laugh or cry."

"So, what are you going to do?" Rachel asked.

"If I knew who or why, I'd do something, but I don't, so I guess I'll have to play it by ear. People get tired of pranks if there's no reaction, don't they?"

"That's what they say."

"Who, Rachel? Why?"

"I wish I knew. Listen, maybe we'll notice someone who's acting weird or, better yet, catch the note sender in the act."

"Yeah. Just keep your eyes and ears open for me."

"Will do," she said with a little salute. Then she looked at her watch. "Say, I'm going to have to get home. I hate to leave you like this, though. Will you be all right? Will Mrs. Pemberton be here soon?"

Maggie Pemberton was the neighbor staying with me part-time while my parents were on their twenty-fifth wedding anniversary trip. Baby-sitting me was more like it, but I'd gone along with it so as not to spoil their special vacation.

"She'll be here in an hour or so. I'll be fine, Rachel. Really."

"Are you going to tell her about this note thing?"

"I doubt it," I replied. Mrs. Pemberton was like an aunt to Mom, and I loved her like family, but things people told her had a way of slipping out.

Rachel nodded as we walked down the stairs. "I still think Paris would be more romantic than Italy."

"Huh? Oh, you mean the trip. Me, too. It's just that Mom majored in art history in college, and since Italian Renaissance paintings were her area of focus, she's just always wanted to go to Italy. Dad's been a Roman architecture nut for almost as long."

"Well, that does sound cool. Listen, I'll see you at school in the morning. Call me if you need to talk. It'll all work out, Katie."

"I will. Thanks for being here."

Back in my room, wanting to keep busy, I checked the assignment sheet that had started this whole thing. Monday: Breen's assignment was due on Monday. I'd have to let Rachel know.

I did three geometry problems, but when my eyes kept straying to the wastebasket, I knew it was going to be impossible to concentrate. I finally gave up, reached into the wicker basket, smoothed out the balled-up piece of paper, and read those awful words again.

They had almost as much electricity in them as they had the first time, but now I knew I wasn't going to pass out. No, I wanted to smash something. The nerve of this person! Me and Grayson? Why me? Why him?

Think, Katie, I told myself, but I just drew a blank. Had anybody acted strange that day? I remembered Mark Sherman hiccupping nonstop most of third period. That had been different but totally unrelated to the note. And a fire drill that afternoon had freaked out Gaby Slocum. Then there was the overall somberness during choir practice, but given the circumstances, even that had been pretty normal.

When had the person had the opportunity to sneak the message into my notebook, anyway? When it came right down to it, I realized it could have been done in a split second during almost any of my classes or the fire drill, at choir practice, or even when my papers had gone flying all over the hallway after school.

That had happened when Rachel and I were in front of my locker as I rummaged through a notebook for a biology diagram she wanted to see. Her eyes had zeroed in on a piece of paper with little hearts and my writing all over it.

"Katie . . . Dumont?" she quizzed.

"Give me that! Come on, Rachel, I don't want anyone to see it."

"Yeah, especially not Paul Dumont," she teased. "Hey, speak of the devil."

"Paul? Oh no! Is he coming this way?" My heart did a strange little dance whenever he was in the vicinity, and it was really cha-chaing at the moment. When she nodded, I grabbed the page out of her hand, and that's when my books and stuff had gone flying all over.

"Just act nonchalant," she said as I hid the telltale heart-decorated paper and we stooped to gather my things.

One-two-cha-cha-cha. Was he coming? "Here, let me help." My heartbeat slowed.

"Hi, Jason," I greeted as he bent down to help. I did a quick survey. Paul had disappeared. I sighed just as Rachel poked me in the ribs.

"Um, Rachel Stamm, this is Jason Porter. Jason, Rachel just moved here from Seattle."

"Nice town," he commented as he looked at her appreciatively.

"Hi. Oregon's nice, too."

They were still scoping each other out when Mr. Grayson walked up. I blushed now to even think of him, but at the time—*just a couple of hours ago,* I thought with amazement—*seeing him hadn't meant a thing.*

He smiled as he held out my pen and a couple of papers. "I think you dropped these, too."

"Thanks."

And that had been it, almost. After I had given Rachel the biology diagram, we'd run into Elena.

"Would you wait here just a sec, Rachel? Elena?" I called. I knew she heard me by the way her body tensed. "Elena!" But she kept on walking, and I wondered for the hundredth time why it had to be this way between us. I considered running after her, but didn't. Rachel caught up with me. "What's with her?"

"I dunno. Bad day, I guess. Say, did I see some electricity between you and Jason?"

"He's pretty cool," she said as we left the building. That's when we'd gone to my house and found the note.

Why me? I wondered again. I mean, I was so ordinary-looking. Everything about me was so . . . so average: brown hair and eyes, average height and weight. Rachel, on the other hand, was beautiful with her flowing red hair, amber eyes, and a figure to die for.

She was someone the guys really noticed. *Moi?* I was just the girl-next-door type. So why me and not someone drop-dead pretty?

Why and who? Who and why?

Suddenly, I just couldn't stay cooped up in the house. I didn't want to think about the note and, mostly, what it would be like to sit in Mr. Grayson's class the next day, or to walk down the halls at school, wondering if, at any given moment, I was face-to-face with the note sender without even knowing it.

Rachel was all right to talk to, but I'd known her for a grand total of a few weeks.

I wanted my best friend. I wanted Elena. For a second, I remembered the snub in the hallway that afternoon, but somehow this time I would get her to talk to me. That decided, I scribbled a note for Mrs. Pemberton.

As I walked the two blocks to Elena's, memories came flooding back. We'd been two four-year-olds bonded together by a chance meeting at a birthday party our neighbor was throwing for her visiting niece. It was as if Elena and I had become friends the moment we had clasped hands out of mutual fear of Mrs. Briton's electrified bug-zapping screen door.

Tea parties, skinned knees, laughter, and consoling words all blurred together in the complex fabric of a long friendship, and it really hurt that she was shutting me out now. Hadn't I been patient long enough?

I wasn't going to get the chance to think about it any further. Elena stood in her driveway, looking as much like a pixie as ever. That sameness only brought home how different . . . spoiled . . . everything was, and I knew more than ever how much I wanted to get our friendship back onto the right track.

"Elena," I said.

She jumped. When she realized who had called her name, she started to turn away. Was she going to walk out on me without even hearing me out? Having that happen at school was bad enough. I couldn't let her do it on the driveway where we'd ridden tricycles and played hopscotch.

"No, don't go back in." I walked closer and shook my head. "How could it come down to this?"

She just kicked at a little stone for what seemed like the longest time. At least she hadn't gone inside.

"To what?" she finally asked.

"To this! You won't even look at me, let alone have a real conversation with me. You were ignoring me at school, too. Look, I know you're hurting because your parents split. I'm not trying to make light of that. But, Elena, don't shut everyone out. Don't you remember playing Barbies?"

"Yeah."

I wanted to shake her. Didn't all the things from all those years of friendship mean anything to Elena? I tried again with something more recent.

"The false eyelashes?"

"I don't have Alzheimer's."

"You know, I've tried to be patient, to give you time, but Elena, you're starting to drag me down with you, and we all have our limits."

"So, you've written me off. Well, Rachel Stamm is moving right in, isn't she?" Elena's small face was still looking down at the stone. I couldn't decipher her emotions for sure, but it seemed like a combination of fear and anger.

"Rachel's a new friend, yes, but you and I have been best friends since we were preschoolers. Trying to write you off? No way! But I don't know when I last saw you smile. Elena, you can't let your parents' problems wreck your life."

"Well, they are."

"Maybe you need to see someone then."

"See someone? Like a shrink? Isn't that your department? Have you thrown any lamps into your front yard lately?"

Yeah, get me where it hurts, I thought. Well, I didn't have to take it. I started to walk away. Then something stopped me. Her words didn't change all the years behind us. Could I let them ruin our chance for now and the future?

"That's hitting below the belt, Elena Banning. I'm only trying to help you, you know, and what are you doing? You're dredging up stuff that has nothing to do with what we are talking about."

"Okay, okay. I'm sorry I said that, but Katie, please, won't you just butt out?"

"You know, I almost wish I could, but you need a friend, and I need one, too, especially right now. Just hear me out and then I'll leave. Look, Kiddie," I said in a softer voice, using our childhood nickname for each other. "I love you like a sister. I used to be able to ease your hurts, and now I can't. This is way too big for a bandage or a few tears. In fact, I can't even know what you're going through this time."

"You can say that again," she put in.

"Anyway, I'm here for you. I still need you in my life, and deep down, I think you still need me. Please, please try to climb out of that shell, Elena.

"I'm going now."

For a moment, I fantasized that she'd come running to me and say all the things we both needed to get our friendship moving ahead again, but she didn't, and when I started walking down the driveway, away from her, my heart felt like lead.

Day 2
Wednesday

Mr. Grayson's classroom was just as it had been the day before, but everything seemed so different today, so charged somehow, with my awareness of him. A "thing" with my second-period teacher?

"Good morning," he greeted everyone as he strode into the room with his usual brisk vitality. His voice vibrated through me in a new, personalized way that I didn't want or like.

Nothing's really changed, I reminded myself

"I have your essays," he said as he waved a sheaf of papers. "For the most part, I was very impressed by your descriptive powers. One of you, for instance, described his dog as having 'nickel-sized' paws. Another of you wrote of a church with 'lily pad green' windows. Those images do much to make a reader really see the object of description."

When he stopped to read from a couple of the essays, I thought how, if we are guilty of labeling people, my tag for him had been good teacher. All right, to be honest, maybe it had been good-looking good teacher. I mean, you'd have to be half-dead not to notice that he happened to be cool.

Not only did he have a fantastic build, but so early in the school year, his sun-bleached hair and the sprinkle of freckles across his nose made him look even cooler, sort of like a little towheaded boy who had grown up just right. When I came to the ocean-colored eyes, I knew I didn't want to look right into them. Not today. Would he be able to tell something weird had happened?

" . . . Katie?" The sound of his voice saying my name turned something in my knees and cheeks to ice. This was terrible. I couldn't let some stupid prank do this to me. Still, the direct communication with him so soon after the note made me want to vanish. Maybe I was going to, because I felt so cold and detached, like I was drifting away. Then his voice pulled me back to reality.

"Katie, you did a notable job of describing a small town in your 'Portrait of a Tired Lady.' I'd like to share a couple of passages with the class, if I may."

I nodded.

There was something so normal about the way he read my words that it broke the ice. He was just Mr. Grayson, my teacher, again. Everything would be all right. The rest of the class seemed to go a lot more easily.

Afterwards, just outside the room, Rachel was waiting for me.

"Did you see anyone acting weird?" I asked.

"Everybody," she joked. Then she got serious. "No, not really."

"Me, either."

"Well, you got through it fine."

"It didn't feel that way, especially when he called my name. I thought I would faint, Rachel. I mean, I almost lost it right there in front of everybody."

"It didn't show," she assured me. "Let's talk more after school. I've got to get to the other end of the building."

"Geometry for me." I made a little face. I'd done my problems pretty half-heartedly the night before. "And I do need to talk more about it. Call me tonight. I have choir after school."

"Talk to you later." She gave my arm a little squeeze, and I was glad all over again that we had clicked as friends.

During lunch, although I suppose I was keeping up my end of the conversation, an uncustomary self-consciousness wormed into my being. The things that normally interested me didn't. Maren and Laura, for example, went on and on about a big fall sale at Nordstrom's that I might have been interested in, but wasn't. Was a dumb prank even going to change the way I interacted with my friends? I even forgot to look for Paul Dumont.

Instead, I felt strangely alone in the big, people-filled room.

People: maybe that was it. Was one of them playing games with me? Was he or she watching even as I ate and talked with my friends? A little shiver went through me, but nobody noticed.

Although I might have told Maren and Laura about the note business, I just didn't feel like sharing it with them, at least not yet. I wished Rachel didn't have second lunch.

I wished even more that Elena were sitting here with us, as she used to last year in ninth grade. I could see her in a corner of the room, picking at her food. She looked so lost right then that I had this awful, sudden feeling that she might do something stupid.

Maren must have noticed me staring at Elena.

"She's really down," she commented, nodding in Elena's direction.

"I know."

"You're her best friend," Laura said. "Has she shut you out, too?"

"Yeah."

"What can we do?" Laura asked. The four of us had palled around together since seventh grade, but now Elena had become her own little island, floating in a sea of people who cared. When I spoke again to my friends—Elena's friends—it was with feeling.

"I wish I knew. I've tried to be supportive, tried to get through to her, but she's so closed-off that I'm getting absolutely nowhere. I'm really worried about her."

"It's so unlike her," Maren put in. I knew what she meant. Normally, Elena was one of the most congenial people I knew.

"Hey," Laura suggested, "how about going to Ms. Daniels about her?"

"That's not a bad idea," I said, thinking of Tanisha Daniels, the school counselor whom we all liked and respected. "I'm not sure it's good timing, though. Elena's supposed to solo at Mr. Soderquist's memorial service on Saturday."

"Yeah, it might not be good to rattle her right before," Laura agreed, and Maren nodded.

"What's Tyler's take on Elena's attitude, Laura?" I asked. If anyone knew, Laura probably would, since she had been a pretty steady item with Elena's brother before the Bannings' separation and Tyler's move.

"I still think it's a crime that they split Elena and Tyler up," Maren said with a toss of her long, lion-colored hair.

So did I, and I suspected that being separated from her brother was part of Elena's problem now. Born only thirteen months apart, they'd been more like twins than any other brother and sister I knew.

"Well, naturally," Laura informed us, "he's worried about her and their mom. It's really hard on Mrs. Banning, from what he's told me, especially since she's Catholic and all. She's sort of shut herself down."

"Which probably means Elena isn't getting much support from her," Maren said.

"Right," Laura seconded.

"Her mom must be hurting," I said. I had known Elena's mother for so long that I was familiar with her strong faith and Guatemalan ancestry, and I knew she didn't believe in divorce. It must have ripped her apart when her husband had decided he'd had enough of the marriage and then taken their son with him to California. But I also Steven Banning and knew there were two sides to every story. I didn't want to make judgments about their situation. I wanted only to help their daughter.

"Well, let's see how it goes after the memorial service," Maren suggested. "If Elena doesn't snap out of this soon, I think Ms. Daniels might be able to get through where we can't."

We all decided that that would be our plan of action.

"To change the subject," Laura informed us, "Ben Taggart is looking over this way." Maren blushed when he flashed her a special smile. It was a nice, light moment.

Then Laura spoiled it.

"How would you like to see Grayson give you that kind of smile?" she asked. Maren thumped her hand over her heart.

When I laughed along with them, mine rang hollow, and I was glad that lunch period was ending.

I tried hard to bury my uneasy thoughts by concentrating on afternoon classes, and it almost worked. Even so, I had some moments, and one of them came during Mr. Breen's class.

"How far do we go with free speech?" he asked as part of a discussion on the Bill of Rights. "What is your interpretation of 'free speech,' off the top of your head?

Anyone? Rachel?"

"Well, I think we have the right to say what we think and feel, but I think we also have to let our consciences guide us. We shouldn't go around saying things that will deliberately belittle or hurt others."

When her eyes strayed over to me, I knew she was thinking about the note as well as the larger issue.

Was a note an example of free speech? Did the anonymous louse have the right to accuse me of doing something with my teacher? What gave him or her the right to upset me the way this was upsetting me? What about my rights? Well, at least no one else seemed to know about it. I didn't even want to think what it might be like if a rumor got started. Gossip, I knew, was free speech, and too many people automatically believed smoke meant fire.

I tried to focus away from the note topic. "Sean?" I heard Mr. Breen say.

"Yeah, like those neo-Nazi rallies."

"But they are legal," Jake Weiner put in. "Sad to say. I'm sure the Founding Fathers didn't envision anything like Hitler and the Nazis."

"Ah, or maybe they did, Jake. Maybe they did, in a way. Think about that, and we'll take it up tomorrow."

The rest of the school day, if poignant, looked up— way up.

Choir practice was emotional on the heels of our director's death. It wasn't as if we hadn't been expecting it since Mr. Soderquist had had terminal cancer. In fact, he had suffered so that his death was one of those blessing-type things. Still, as his replacement led us through the choral tribute we were to present at the memorial service, it was impossible not to remember the man with a lump in my throat. "Our own 'Mr. Holland,' some people had said in reference to the movie. Whatever, Mr. Soderquist had loved music, people, and life. He had touched people for the better.

"Let's make him proud on Saturday," Mr. Wagner said with feeling.

The new Elena darted out the second choir practice was over, and I thought how ironic it was that Mr. Soderquist had died so full of life, while Elena was so physically alive and yet in some ways so dead. It helped to have the Tanisha Daniels plan in mind, but I was still shaking my head at the irony when none other than Paul Dumont, who sang tenor, walked up to me.

I was going to faint!

"Are you saying no before I even ask?" he quizzed playfully. Then he flashed me a smile that turned my knees to jelly. What got me wasn't the beautiful teeth as much as the way the smile made his hazel eyes crinkle so warmly. I tried to act casual, but my heart was doing its funny little cha-cha.

"Hi, Paul. I must have been a million miles away."

"Well, were you?"

"Was I?"

"Turning me down."

"I'd never say 'no' without knowing the question," I said. I wasn't a flirt by nature. Was this flirting? Was I saying the right things? I mean, this was the coolest junior at Oak Meadow. Nervously, I twisted my locket on its chain.

"It's really odd—sad odd— to be rehearsing this service, isn't it?" he asked as he touched his thick, chestnut-colored hair.

I'd been thinking about Mr. Soderquist myself, but from our banter, Paul's question wasn't what I had expected, and my dream of something more started to evaporate.

"Yeah, he was really special."

"Anyway, the question I was referring to," he said as

hope sprang back into my heart, "had something to do with Mr. Soderquist, in a way. I was remembering the Swing Into Spring Concert and the way you didn't think those old numbers were silly and old-fashioned.

"Do you really like Cole Porter and the Gershwins?"

"Like them? I'm crazy about them, Paul." I'd even coaxed Grandpa Krieg into making tapes of his old records, but I didn't want to overdo it by coming on too strong.

"Great! Well, it's like this. My parents bought some tickets to a 30s and 40s concert at the Schnitz, only they aren't going to be able to make it. I was wondering if you'd like to go with me on Friday."

And that was it. He'd asked me out! Paul Dumont had actually asked me out on a date! It seemed like the most incredible thing, and on my way home, I hummed a medley of oldies.

"My, you're in a good mood," Mrs. Pemberton said with a laugh as I kissed her cheek on the way into the kitchen. "Did you have a good day?"

The funny thing was, it had been a lousy day, mainly, and then Paul Dumont had magically transformed it. The note business was dead, without any harm other than stress to me, and my dream guy had finally asked me out.

"The greatest," I told her. She was rolling out the crust for a pie. "Is that going to be lemon?"

"Lemon it is."

"My favorite."

I stayed in the kitchen long enough to listen to what had happened between Nikki and Victor on her favorite soap opera, and with Desdemona, her feisty Burmese cat.

Desdemona was the reason Mrs. Pemberton was coming to our house, instead of my just staying with her, since Des and my Pomeranian, Cognac, despised each other. Cognac, at 15, was getting a little crotchety, and Des had a talent for taking a swipe at her nose and inciting a mini-war. So, Mrs. Pemberton shuffled back and forth from my house to hers.

After dinner, I breezed through my homework. It was all I could do not to call Rachel, but I decided to savor the anticipation of the moment I would tell her that Paul had asked me out.

Finally, the phone rang. "Any more notes," she started the conversation.

"Thank goodness, no. I really think it was a one-time thing."

"I'll keep my fingers crossed."

"Something did happen just after choir practice."

"Something happened? What kind of thing? You're not being stalked or anything now, are you?"

"No, no, no," I laughed. "Nothing like that. Nothing even remotely like that. Rachel, Paul Dumont asked me out!"

"Where did that come from? You must be floating. Tell me how it happened?" When I did, she asked if I really liked those silly songs.

"They're not silly. They're wonderful," I corrected.

"You're in love."

And maybe I was. All I know is that I fell asleep thinking not of awful notes, as I had the night before, but of one dreamy junior.

I can't say that I went to school the next morning without a care in the world—the *who* and *why* behind the note remained maddeningly unanswered—but things looked a whole lot brighter than they had the previous morning.

Paul Dumont had me on a high that floated me right to my locker, and maybe it's partly because I was so up that the paper sticking through the air vent in the metal door brought me down the way it did.

It can't be, I thought.

Instead of pulling the sheet through, I decided to unlock the door and reach the page from within, for more privacy. Let it be a message from Rachel, Maren, or Laura, I begged the powers-that-be as I fumbled with my combination. My fingers felt so stiff that I had to go through the series of numbers four times. It was weird to feel so rattled while everyone around me casually went about the business of opening lockers and taking out books. Just days ago, I'd taken that luxury for granted, too. And now I was shaking, just trying to get mine open.

There! I finally had it. As I eased the panel open, the paper fluttered to my feet. I left it there momentarily as I stuck some books onto a shelf That's right: stall, Katie.

When I picked it up, it was with a sinking feeling that I saw the same kind of paper, complete with pucker marks. Still, something inside me kept telling me that it couldn't be another note.

With the door as a shield, I slowly unfolded it, and the pasted-on alphabet letters jumped out at me:

iS GRaySON a
GOOD KiSSeR?

It just blew my mind that this was happening for a second time. Such a wave of dizziness hit that I had to lean forward and put my head against the metal shelf to steady myself

"What are you doing in there?" I heard Rachel ask. "Swooning over Paul?"

I was going to vomit.

"I've gotta go to the restroom, Rachel. I feel sick." Then I ran. About the time my breakfast came up, I heard the tardy bell ring.

Rachel came in as I was wiping my forehead with a wet paper towel. She knew right away.

"You got another one, didn't you?"

"Yeah."

"Are you going to be okay? Do you want me to call the school nurse or someone?"

"No, please don't do that, because then I'd have to explain, and I don't want to get into it."

"Is it that bad?" she asked.

"What? I suppose not really, but Rachel, it's just the fact that this is continuing like this."

"You know, I know you won't like this," she said, "but I think you have to tell someone, and I think it should start with Mr. Grayson. That is, if this new note mentioned him by name again. Did it?"

"Oh, yeah. But I still don't know about telling him."

"Well, he's involved by name. Turn it around. If your name was on something like this, wouldn't you want to know?"

"I guess."

"Listen, maybe you should get a pass and go home for the day. Think this out.

You can tell the nurse you've got cramps or something."

"Maybe that'd be best," I said, still shaky from the discovery. Then something happened. No, that was what this freaky person wanted. He or she wanted to get me this way, to disrupt my life. Maybe the best thing I could do was go on as normally, at least for appearance's sake, as possible.

"Come on, I'll help you," Rachel offered.

"Thanks, Rachel. No, I'm not going home. I'm going to biology!"

"That's the way to go. But think about telling someone."

"Okay," I promised. Then we were on our way to biology. Mrs. Tucci didn't even make a big thing about our coming in late.

Bravado aside, sitting through another of Mr. Grayson's classes was even harder than it had been yesterday. I mean, a second note . . . One was bad enough, but two meant some kind of pattern didn't it? Would it stop at two?

"In your next essay," he informed the class, "you are going to be using your persuasive skills . . ."

I tuned out momentarily. Maybe Rachel was right.

Maybe he did have the right to know, but how in the world would I tell him? I hate to mess up your day, Mr. Grayson, but by the way, someone is accusing us of having a thing.

"One of my students last year, for example, wrote a letter trying to convince an imaginary daughter to stay in school. Another . . ."

I could tell the principal, but surely she'd get back to Mr. Grayson about it anyway. Why worry him about something so absurd? But then again, what if a rumor got started, and what if Mr. Grayson's knowing could somehow stave off something worse down the line? How would I feel if one day he said, "Katie, why in the world didn't you just come and tell me this was going on? I had every right to know."

"It can be anything," he was telling the class. "It can be a personal conviction or a social issue. Talk someone out of smoking. Persuade the city council to save the woods. The common thread is that it should be something you believe in enough to write about with feeling."

In told, it would be better to go to him directly. Would I want someone to involve a third party if the tables were turned? Mr. Grayson would know what to do, whom to involve.

". . . thinking about your topic, but for now we need to brush up on some basic composition skills. I want these next essays to glow," he said with enthusiasm.

And it was that zest for teaching English that decided me. I'd tell him. I had to. He was such a good teacher. A rumor about this, no matter how ridiculous, could damage his reputation.

At lunch, I felt the note sender's intrusion even more than I had the day before, since it spoiled my special news. Instead of feeling undiluted happiness when I told Maren and Laura about Paul asking me out, my emotions were tinged by the reality of another note and tainted by the dread of knowing I was going to tell Mr. Grayson about it that very afternoon.

It just wasn't fair!

Then during history, I started wondering what Paul would think if he found out I was getting anonymous notes that linked me with a teacher. He barely knew me. Would he believe there was any truth to it? Would it be a reflection on me?

I just didn't need this, especially not now.

I thought the afternoon would never end, and yet I also wanted last period to go on forever. Was I really going to tell Mr. Grayson?

"Let's forget it," I said to Rachel when we met at my locker after school. "You can't. Remember what we talked about? He has a right to know."

"That doesn't make it easy," I said as we walked down the hall toward his office. "Come on, Katie. It won't be that bad. It's not like you're going to the guillotine."

"It feels like I am."

And then we were at his door. It was ajar, but he hadn't seen us yet. We could still leave. What was I going to say, anyway? Maybe I should give this more thought.

"It'll be all right," Rachel whispered, and when I nodded, she knocked.

It was probably a normal-sounding tapping, but to me, it came out like machine gun fire, and my heart thumped hard against my ribs in a matching rat-a-tat-tat. It got even worse when I heard his voice.

"Come in."

Thank goodness Rachel was with me for moral support. Her little nudge reminded me of how necessary this was. *Come on, Katie,* I told myself, *if you can sing a solo in front of a couple hundred people, you can get through this.*

Rachel held the door while I went in first.

"Katie. Rachel. What may I do for you today?" he asked with his usual friendliness from behind his desk. One of the things I liked best about Mr. Grayson was that he was so available to his students; no question was ever too stupid or unimportant.

Why did it have to be such a nice guy? It made it all the harder to tell him.

"We need to talk to you about something important," Rachel prompted. "Do you have a minute?"

"Be my guests." He motioned for us to sit down. "I've had several questions about that essay."

"Um, Mr. Grayson," I ventured, "it isn't about the paper. In fact, I don't know where to start." When I paused, trying to find the right words, I could see his easy expression change to one of mild concern.

"If there's a problem . . ."

"There is," I said, grateful for the opening, "and that's why Rachel is with me."

"Go ahead."

Even though it was warm in his office, I felt my hands ice up.

"Katie?"

When he looked from me to Rachel, I knew I had to tell him. It had to come from me.

"I don't know where to begin," I said again.

"The beginning is usually the best point," he suggested with a little smile.

"Well, it all started with this weird note that I found in one of my school folders.

The reason I'm telling you about it is . . . well . . . in a way it also concerns you."

"Me? In what way?"

"I can't do this!"

"It's all right, Katie. You said a note you'd gotten also concerns me." Momentarily, I looked down at my shoe. Then I looked at his puzzled face and blurted it out.

"It suggested that you and I are more than just a teacher and his student."

"More than . . ." That's as far as he got before his forehead wrinkled into a frown. Then he ran his long fingers through his wheat-colored hair.

"Can you be more explicit? What, exactly, did it say?"

"There were two. I'm not sure the exact words really matter. I just felt that I had to let you know that someone is sending these to me, because of the way your name is on the notes."

"Do you have them with you?" he asked. I nodded.

"I'd like to see them. Since my name is on them, I would like to get a better feel of what's going on."

I could understand that, but somehow letting him see the accusations in that awful chopped-up print would make the situation seem even more terrible. He must have seen my hesitation.

"It's okay," he assured me. "We can handle this."

"I feel so embarrassed, though."

"I understand, but you really needn't. Katie, what somebody else has done is not necessarily a reflection on you . . . or me, either, for that matter."

"Okay," I told him as I reached for my backpack. When I lifted the flap, everything seemed like some bizarre dream, like I was moving through molasses.

Then the feel of the crisp edges of the papers made everything all too real again. I pulled the notes out and handed them to my teacher.

His face paled as he read first one message and then the other. Silent as the seconds ticked by, he absorbed their meaning. Then he looked at me.

"Well, you and I know this is hogwash. Tell me again when and how you found this garbage."

I did.

"And you don't have any idea who is doing this?"

"No. I've gone over and over it, and I keep drawing a blank."

"Since the note composer has connected us in this way, apparently it's someone who knows us both. Someone, perhaps, in our comp class. Katie, other than Rachel, does anyone else know about this?"

"As far as I know, just the note sender."

"That's good to know. Have you gotten any strange phone calls? E-mail? Has anything else unusual happened?"

"No."

"Then let's sit on this, Katie, and hope this is the end of it. I'm glad you told me.

I trust that you will let me know if you receive anything further. Will you do that?"

"I will," I promised.

"Whew! I'm relieved that that's over," I said to Rachel later over pizza.

"Aren't you glad we went now?"

"Yeah, mostly, except that now he's worried, too."

"But I think he appreciated being told."

"I suppose." I shook my head. "Why would anybody do this to us, Rachel?"

"You've got me there," she shrugged. "Hey, let's brainstorm."

"Sounds good to me, but where do we start? I mean, it's those old questions: Who? Why?"

"Okay, let's treat this like a crime. You know, like they

do on television with a murder or something. What would a detective ask? How about, 'Do you have any enemies?'"

"Yeah, I guess that's where they start. Hmm. Enemies?"

"Maybe that's too strong a word. How about, 'Is there anyone, ma'am, who might hold a grudge against you? Can you think of anyone you might have hurt or made angry lately?'"

"That's the thing, Rachel. I can't."

"Oh, come on. Sure you can. There's always someone, like a guy you brushed off, maybe, or a friend who's been acting differently. Stuff like that."

The funny thing was, when she put it that way, I could. I thought of Sharon Fleming. We'd never been very close, but she'd been acting weird toward me ever since I'd beaten her out in choir try-outs. Then there was Todd Glanders. But I didn't want to start naming names. And anyway, I couldn't imagine Sharon or Todd doing this. The brainstorming wasn't going very well, and I felt more depressed than ever.

"Sure, I can think of a few things, but Rachel, even if someone really hated me—and the people I thought of really have no reason to hate me—why involve Mr. Grayson?"

I didn't expect Rachel's reaction. She laughed. "Probably because he's such a hunk." she said.

"I suppose he is, but he's a teacher."

"Even teachers can make you drool. That butt . . ."

"Rachel!"

"Don't tell me you haven't noticed."

I wanted to tell her that, no, I hadn't, but lately . . . lately . . .

"Whether or not he's cute is beside the point," I said.

"It's better than being accused of being involved with Mr. Breen."

I broke out laughing. I mean, I don't believe in making fun of people for the way they look, but Mr. Breen had the awfullest beetle brows and black hair growing out of his nose.

Worst of all, he got so excited when he was talking about historical topics that sometimes he spit.

"More to drink?" The waitress interrupted just then.

"Sure," we told her in unison.

"Where were we?" Rachel asked after we had our refills.

"Just a sec," I said as I leaned over to get something out of my backpack. I got what I needed. "Mr. Breen."

"At least I made you laugh."

"Yeah, but he's a really nice teacher." I took a swig of soda.

"What was that?" Rachel asked.

"I just said . . ."

"No, you know. That was a pill you just took, and it didn't look like an aspirin." I'd popped it into my mouth and swallowed it without thinking, in between a bite of food and our conversation. Right then, I really missed that easy, familiar way Elena and I had. Had had, I sadly amended to myself. Well, this was Rachel, not Elena. I could tell her it was a vitamin or an allergy pill, I guessed. Why did I have to get into this stupid pill business with a friend I was just getting to know? "Oh," I hedged, "it's sort of complicated. Let's talk about Jason."

"Well, uncomplicate it for me." Then something seemed to click in her mind. She bored her amber eyes into me. "Katie, you're not on something, are you?"

"Oh, no, not in the way I think you mean."

"Well? Is it a tranquilizer because of this weird situation?"

"Okay. Like I said, it's sort of complicated. See, I had encephalitis when I was little and have this seizure disorder thing that I take medicine for."

"Gross! Isn't that like some kind of brain disease?"

"Yeah. That's why I need the medicine. The encephalitis messed up something in my brain. You mean, it's taken you this long to notice what a weirdo I am?" I added, trying to make light of it, but she wasn't ready to let it go.

"What happens if you don't take it?"

"I do strange things I can't help or control."

"Strange things? Like what?" she asked.

"Are you sure you really want to hear this?"

"Well, yeah. Is it making you feel funny to talk about it?"

"A little." What an understatement.

"But we spend a lot of time together. What if something happens? Maybe I should know about it?"

"Hmm. Yeah, that makes sense. Well, to put it in a nutshell, the electrical currents in my brain get messed up without the medicine, or without even the right dose of it."

"Okay, I'm following you, but what happens? You said something about things you can't help."

"All right. Once this flashing, pulsating strobe light went off. It triggered something in my brain—this was before I was on the right dose of medicine—and I don't remember anything. I know I do things because of what I see later . . . like something I've thrown. All I know is that some time passes when I'm not really aware."

Oh great, now she probably thought I was some kind of nut case. But when she spoke, she seemed more interested than judgmental, and I relaxed a bit.

"What if you forgot your medicine?" she asked.

"Probably not much would happen if I missed a dose or two. Sometimes I have when I've had the flu and not been able to keep it down. But I'm not going to test it out!"

"Is that why you didn't want to see that video? Or go to Haber's?" Haber's was a seventies-style place to dance that featured pulsating lights in a rainbow of colors.

"Yeah, exactly. Even with the medicine in my system, I need to avoid certain kinds of special light effects."

"Well, you'd never know it."

"Thanks. I don't try to hide it, but it's not something you want to go around broadcasting, either. People are still in the Dark Ages about epilepsy and seizure disorders."

"Yeah, well I'm glad I know." Then suddenly she switched the conversation by asking, "Tell me about Elena."

"What do you mean?" As glad as I was to get off the topic of my anticonvulsant medication, I didn't quite know where she was coming from now.

"I thought she was your best friend or something. She doesn't act very tight with you now." I didn't comment right away. "Well, if you don't want to talk about it."

"It's not that I don't want to share things," I said. "I've known Elena since before we started school. It's just that she's going through a bad time right now. She's not herself"

"Boy, you're naive."

"Naive? How?"

"From the way she snubs you, Katie, it's obvious she doesn't want to be your friend. I mean, friendships die, you know. They go boom in some argument or they just fizzle out."

Was mine with Elena dying? The thought made something tighten in my throat. Dying? No, it wasn't like Rachel said.

"What you say about friendships dying is true, but she's been my friend for so long that I owe it to Elena, and to myself, to give it some time and not jump to conclusions."

"It's weird you two even ended up friends."

"How so?"

"Well, she's Mexican or something."

"Actually, she's as American as we are. She gets her coloring and name from her Guatemalan grandmother."

"Oh."

When the topic switched from Elena to guys, I was as happy about the change as I had been when we had stopped discussing my medicine.

In my room that night, I wondered if Rachel might be a little jealous of my longtime friendship with another girl.

Whatever, the crazy, mixed-up day had exhausted me. I think I must have fallen asleep as soon as my head hit the pillow.

Day 4
Friday

"Buon giorno!"

"Mom! You sound like you're calling from Seattle, not Italy."

Then I felt sort of queasy. What if they were calling on their way home? Had they found out about the note business somehow? It would be just like them to overreact and cancel the rest of their trip.

"Where are you today, anyway?" I asked. Let it be Italy, I prayed.

"Sorrento," Mom said as I breathed a sigh of relief, "and it's absolutely glorious.

We have the most splendid view from our hotel room of the quaint little fishing harbor far below. And Dad says to tell you that we survived driving along the Amalfi Coast. The drop is straight down, but the view from the narrow road that snakes along the cliff edge, if perilous, is a postcard scene."

"I can hardly wait to see your slides."

Then Dad got on the phone and described their stay

in Rome. "What did you like best there?" I asked.

"Hmm. It's a little like comparing apples and oranges, Katie, but you know my penchant for Roman architecture, so I think I'd have to say the Forum. Rome is such an impressive, vital city, and you just never know what you'll chance upon around the next corner. It can be anything from the little theater where Caesar was assassinated to a bridge flanked by huge Bernini statues."

"The Eternal City," I mused. Then my thoughts strayed. It didn't seem quite right to let them think everything at home was fine.

"It really is that," Dad agreed. "Mom wants back on."

"We're saving the best for last," she told me as she excitedly ran down her list of must-sees in Florence and the rest of Tuscany. "We are planning to have our anniversary dinner in the castle on the itinerary sheet."

"That sounds so romantic. An anniversary in a real castle . . ."

If I had had any thoughts about telling my parents about the harassment, Mom's breathless enthusiasm over the last leg of their dream trip quashed them. It could wait until they got home.

"I'm just fine," I assured them, which was true, in a manner of speaking. "Mom, you'll never guess what."

"What?"

"I still can't believe it, but Paul Dumont asked me out. He's just the coolest guy at Oak Meadow."

"Isn't he the dreamboat who brought the house down at the spring concert?"

"Yeah, that was Paul. I hope it's all right if I go to a concert with him tonight." Mom said something to Dad, and I held my breath during their brief exchange.

They wouldn't say no, would they? When she spoke, I allowed myself to breathe again.

"You go and have a good time. We'll look forward to meeting Paul once we are home. Dad's reminding me that this is long distance."

"It's about time to leave for school, anyway. And, Mom, thanks for letting me go tonight."

"Have a good day, dear."

"Sure, and you two have a wonderful trip. Happy anniversary. Don't forget to open my card on your day."

"Thanks. We won't forget. Would you put Maggie on for a second?" she asked.

"Okay. She's right here. I'm glad you called." Then I turned the phone over to Mrs. Pemberton.

They were checking up on me, I knew, but as I left the house, I smiled. It felt good just then to still be their little girl.

"I think I'll take the chicken fajitas," I told the waiter.

Paul winked at me with those dreamy eyes as if to tell me I'd made a good choice.

Then he ordered Combination Four for himself

"I'm glad you like Mexican," he commented as he ate a chip. "Let's see, so far we've got music and food in common. What else? Do you have brothers and sisters?"

"Two older brothers. Eric is in grad school, studying astrophysics, and Michael, who lives in Indianapolis with his wife, is an accountant. What about you?"

"It sounds like they have some serious math genes."

I laughed. "You know it. In fact, they got them all."

"I'll bet you're better at math than you think. Anyway, I have two older sisters. Jennifer is a freshman at Lewis and Clark College, and Melissa, who lives in Sacramento with her husband, is an R.N. It's because of Melissa, actually, that we're going to the concert tonight. They were my parents' tickets, but Missy just had a baby, and my parents went down."

"Oh, that's great. They must be thrilled. Is it a boy or a girl?"

"A little girl: Haley Marie."

"That's pretty. Say, that makes you Uncle Paul."

"Uncle Paul," he repeated, beaming at the sound of his new status. He told me that he would be flying to California to see Haley for himself the next day. "She's one special little one. All babies are, but Missy lost two before Haley, and it was touch-and-go even with her."

I raised my water glass in a toast. "Here's to Haley Marie, then."

"Haley Marie. Cheers!" he said as we clicked glasses.

The waiter brought our entrées, and we continued talking as we ate. Most of it was the usual small talk between people getting to know each other, but this was Paul Dumont, and everything I heard seemed special. It got even more so about halfway through our meal when he began really showing me who he was, such as in his impassioned defense of trees.

". . . and," he was saying, "it just does something to me deep down inside—it almost hurts, Katie—when they cut those old-growth trees. I know the loggers need their jobs to feed their families, but haven't they stopped to think that there's only a finite number of the big ones left? Are they going to have jobs if they cut, cut, cut? And what happens to our planet if we don't see the larger picture and respect all of nature? Why, already we've created flood and landslide situations because of indiscriminate logging. We just can't go on this way, ruining habitats and stuff. If we do, we may end up being as endangered as the spotted owls."

Wow! He really cared. So many guys just went on and

on about themselves that it was great to hear someone talk about issues that really meant something.

"I couldn't agree more," I said emphatically.

"A girl after my own heart." His warm smile made me glad I'd worn my new persimmon sweater set. I smiled back as he took another bite of enchilada.

"Do you plan a career as a forester?" I asked.

"I'm not sure about that, but I would like to do something to wake people up, maybe get into law or politics, or both. What about you?"

"Well, I get really steamed when towns tear down their vintage buildings without a thought. Some of them are so beautiful and unique. I know a building isn't important in the same way as the ecosystem, but I think the past teaches us so much about the present and leads the way to the future. It's not that I don't like new things, and some old buildings just can't be saved, but I'd like to see more people respect them and at least try. "I see myself down the road as a museum curator or archivist or something else connected with the preservation of the past."

"To the past, then," he said in a new toast.

"And to a future that includes plenty of old-growth trees."

He talked about soccer, and I told him about my parents' trip. Then we got onto the subject of school, which cast a shadow over the carefree meal.

". . . and I have Grayson for junior lit," he finished his list of classes.

I don't know what made me ask the question, but I did. "How do you like him?"

"Grayson?"

"Yeah."

"He's great. He knows the literature, of course, but what I admire is the way he puts himself into it. His class is so alive."

"Yeah, he's great for comp, too." Paul's high estimation of Mr. Grayson did something to me. I'd better snap out of it. I couldn't let Paul know my name was linked with his junior lit teacher's, could I? What was I supposed to say? Paul, I'm in the middle of a situation that might explode in scandal. Nope, it wouldn't do. It wouldn't do at all. He was watching me. I had to get away from the Grayson topic before I gave something away.

"Mr. Breen certainly has a lot of enthusiasm, too," I said.

"That's the truth. Oh, here comes the waiter with the check. It's good timing.

We'd better get going."

And then we had a couple of wonderful hours listening to a rich procession of oldies. At one point during a softer song, Paul reached over and took my hand. For the rest of the concert, he caressed it gently every now and then as little tingles radiated through me.

In the car after the concert, naturally we hummed some of the fabulous tunes fresh in our minds.

"I'll bet you like Broadway musicals, too," Paul commented.

"Most of them are really great," I agreed. "I especially like the old Rodgers and Hammerstein ones."

"We're in sync there. Do you have a favorite?"

"Hmm. It's a hard choice. From the standpoint of music, I think it'd have to be South Pacific, but there are so many wonderful songs from others. Wow, it's a hard choice."

"I think I could second your nomination, but I agree that their other musicals feature some slam-bang songs. Such as: '"Getting to know you,'?" he sang. Then he motioned as if to turn the microphone over to me. [1]

"'Getting to know all about you,'" I picked up.

"'Getting to like you,'" he continued.

"'Getting to hope you like me,'" I sang.

Then in unison we finished: "'Because of all the beautiful and new things I'm learning about you day by day'".

It was so corny that I almost broke out laughing, but at the same time, it was so romantic that my heart was singing a thousand melodies at once. I wanted to put the feeling into my pocket and keep it there forever.

Paul did the laughing for me. Then he got more serious.

"We'd have done Mr. Soderquist proud with that rendition," he said.

"If he can hear us, he's clapping. You are a wonderful tenor."

"Thanks. We're wonderful together."

Then in the dark of the car, he reached for my hand again, and his touch was as tender as a Cole Porter love song.

Of course, they say that something too good to be true probably is. I seemed to go from very high to very low in the blink of an eye these days, and when I grew quiet on the way home, Paul sensed the change in me.

"Are you all right?" he asked.

"Sure, I'm fine."

"You were thinking about Mr. Soderquist, I'll bet."

"I was," I said, which was the truth, in part. The rest was that for some reason, the thought of Mr. Grayson and the notes flitted through my thoughts again and cast a cloud over everything. What was wrong with me that I was letting it do this to me? Instead of the bright, bubbly half of a romantic duo, I suddenly felt like a total dud.

"But?" he coaxed. He really seemed to care.

Should I tell him about the situation, or would he think I had invited it some way?

Did I want to get into that and chance spoiling such a perfect evening? Or would the real spoiling of it come through my clamming up after we'd been so open?

I felt so angry at that anonymous creep for intruding!

But the creep was out there in some kind of void, and Paul Dumont was alive, vital, right next to me. I wouldn't, couldn't, let some nebulous someone ruin things.

"Oh, it's just a problem that gnaws at me now and then," I explained. "It pops into my thoughts for no reason at all at the oddest times."

"If you want to share it with me, I'm a good listener. Hey, don't forget I'm the guy who gets all choked up over sad songs."

"You are, aren't you?" I said, wondering if he'd heard the warmth in my voice.

All I knew was that it didn't matter at all. We had connected on some special level tonight, and suddenly I did want to share.

"Well," I began, "the long and short of it is that I'm being harassed. It's not like some kind of mad stalker is after me, so don't worry, but I'm getting these anonymous notes, and they sort of creep me out."

"I don't blame you. Have you told anyone about it?"

"Yes, but so far there's not much anybody can do. It's sort of a wait and watch situation, and we're hoping it will just fizzle out. But in the meantime, it's unnerving."

"It must be. They haven't threatened your safety, have they? You know, you should go to the police if that happens."

"I know. No, it's not like that. It's more a matter of messages designed to get under my skin."

"Well, you let me know if I can do anything."

"I will. And Paul?"

"Hmm?"

"Thank you."

When he dropped me off, he walked me to the front door. "I had a wonderful time," I said.

"So did I. We'll do it again."

"I'd like that."

He leaned over and gave me a kiss that might have seemed casual, except that when I looked into those hazel eyes just afterwards, I saw them crinkle warmly . . . just for me . . . .

Something inside me was still blossoming when, as Paul walked back toward his car, I heard him whistling Getting to Know You.

I didn't realize I was humming the same song until I encountered Mrs. Pemberton in the study.

"That's from The King and I, isn't it?" she asked from a wing chair where she'd been reading a novel.

"You're right."

She asked me about the concert. "And how was your date?"

"Really great. We had a wonderful dinner before the concert, and Paul is really nice to know."

"His father's in insurance, isn't he?"

"Yes. Paul, Sr."

She nodded. "I'm glad you had a good time, dear. Oh, before I let you go off to dreamland, I found this taped to the back door. I guess one of your friends left it for you before I got back."

"What is it?" I asked as the gears shifted in my mind. Something from one of my friends, or . . . . Not now, I prayed, fearing the worst. Not now when I'm so happy. Maybe just as bad, what if it was another note and Mrs. Pemberton had read it?

When I looked at her again, though, she didn't seem upset. She did look puzzled.

"Katie?"

"I'm sorry. I was just thinking."

"Young men have been known to do that to us girls," she chuckled. "Here." She handed me a sealed envelope. Good. At least she hadn't read it. I relaxed a little, but only a little.

"Thanks. Did you see who left this? Was anyone leaving the house when you arrived back?"

"No. Why don't you open it, and the mystery will be solved?" she suggested.

"Good idea. I think I'll just take it to my room, though."

"I'm going to read on a bit in this book. Mary Higgins Clark can be impossible to put down."

I told her I hoped it was a good book. Then with a sinking feeling, I walked into my room and closed the door.

"It's not what you think it is," I told myself out loud in a little pep talk. Life wouldn't be that cruel, would it, to ruin such a perfect night?

Reluctant to find out, I lay the envelope on my nightstand, carefully took off my clothes, and slipped into a pair of pajamas. Then I picked up the communique as I got into bed.

Sticks and stones may break my bones, but names will never hurt me, I thought as I carefully lifted the flap and pulled out the piece of typewriter paper. But when I saw the pucker marks, I felt the now-familiar revulsion wash over me, and I wasn't sure that old saying about names not hurting was true.

"This is stupid!"

A surge of anger wiped out my reluctance to open this newest piece of garbage. I wouldn't let this do this to me!

Forcefully, I unfolded the page.

My heart jumped. It wasn't just words this time. The picture so startled me that I turned it upside-down on my comforter, as if it would disappear if I weren't actually looking at it.

Had I really seen what I thought I had? Gingerly, I lifted it and looked again.

I'd never seen anything so explicit. But the worst thing about it—the thing that made it obscene—was his name and mine, in hacked-out, neon-bright letters, over the figures of the man and the woman.

Day 5
Saturday

I had to drag myself out of bed the next morning to get ready for Mr. Soderquist's memorial service. Could I skip it, or was a commitment a commitment? I didn't really have to debate the issue. Mr. Wagner needed my alto and, besides, I wanted to be a part of this last tribute to my old choral director. At least I didn't have to solo.

Cognac nipped at my heels as I walked downstairs.

"Oh, your walk," I said to the Pomeranian apologetically. "It's going to have to be a short one."

"Don't worry," sang out Mrs. Pemberton as she stuck her head around the comer.

"I already took her out." As I grabbed a piece of toast, she told me she'd be back at dinnertime. "I have a friend coming to visit this afternoon from Yakima."

"Have a good time. I'll see you later, then. Thanks again for taking care of Cognac's walk," I said as I patted the dog and hurried out. It wasn't that I was late. I just needed some time to get myself together before standing in front of all those people.

All those eyes . . . Would one pair of them belong to the anonymous someone?

And how could I face Mr. Grayson without thinking of that awful picture? Surely he would be at the service with the other faculty and staff.

Then there was Paul. Dueting to *Getting to Know You*—that whole, wonderful evening—now seemed like a dream within the nightmare this situation was fast becoming. I didn't want him to catch my mood and think our date had been a bomb, but so early in our relationship, I hardly wanted to show him such a sensitive picture, either, or even tell him about it.

I shoved all those thoughts into a far corner of my mind as the service began and I heard the glowing testimony to the person Mr. Soderquist had been.

When it was time to sing, the music became a celebration.

You'd have thought Elena's personal trouble would mess up her voice, but her solo to I Believe was the best I'd ever heard her sing. As I listened to her clear, bell-like soprano hit every note perfectly, I wondered if my old friend felt the song's uplifting message of hope and purpose.

I hope so, Kiddie, I thought as I renewed my vow to get through to her.

Then we were singing *This is My Country* just the way Mr. Soderquist had taught us for the spring concert.

As Paul finished the choral tribute with Danny Boy, I thought I was going to fall off the platform as I caught a glimpse of Mr. Grayson and the image in the picture sprang to mind. Had all those people seen my face go from its normal color to bright tomato? Look away, I commanded myself.

When I did, I saw Mrs. Soderquest dabbing her eyes

with a handkerchief, and the purpose of my being there came back with a thud as guilt washed over me. What was the matter with me that I was letting this get to me to the point of intruding upon a heartfelt song in memory of such a nice person? The choir all knew and liked Mrs. Soderquist.

Focusing away from Mr. Grayson, I decided I would write her a note letting her know how glad I was that my life and her husband's had crossed.

Then it was over. As we filed out, Paul caught up with me.

"Your solo was perfect," I told him.

"Thanks. So was our duet. I wish I didn't have to leave this weekend."

"Me, too."

"Me an uncle!" he exclaimed in wonder. "Listen, I've got to run. I'll call you when I get back."

"I'll look forward to that. Have fun getting to know your new little niece."

"Will do," he called as he smiled and dashed toward the door. I knew he had a plane to catch.

When I looked for Elena, she was nowhere in sight. I also didn't see Mr. Grayson again as I left the building.

I walked home with the idea of getting the weekend's homework out of the way . . . if I could concentrate, that is.

The phone was ringing as I walked in.

"I'm going to have to cancel out for tonight," Rachel said.

"Oh, that's okay. Our going to the movies was sort of iffy. I'm not sure I'm up for it anyway."

"Well, I know Maren and Laura are still planning to go. Katie, Jason Porter asked me out!" she announced.

"Oh, Rachel, that's great. Tell me how it happened?"

She did, which led to my telling her the bare basics of my evening with Paul. Then she asked if I wanted to go to the mall with her to find something special to wear on her date.

We'd had some fun times shopping. All of a sudden, though, I felt so tired, so weighed down by wondering how to deal with the third note. Worst of all, would there be still others? No, I didn't feel like going through the motions of a carefree afternoon at Washington Square.

"I think I'll pass, but I saw a lightweight sweater in your favorite apple green at Meier and Frank's."

"Thanks for the tip. Hey, is everything all right? Oh, that's stupid of me. You just got back from that memorial service, didn't you?"

"Yeah." Rachel hadn't known Mr. Soderquist, so there wasn't much to say about that. Instead, I told her I expected a prompt recap of her date, and then we hung up. I would tell her about the note later, when she wasn't on such a cloud about Jason, and after I'd figured out what to do next.

I had barely turned around before the phone rang again.

"Hi again," I said, thinking it was Rachel calling back. But it wasn't Rachel. A shock-wave crackled from my ear down to my toes at the sound of the masculine voice.

"Hello, Katie, it's Mr. Grayson," he said. I tried to pull myself together.

"Oh, I'm sorry, I thought you were my friend calling back, Mr. Grayson?"

"That's all right. I'm calling because I wondered if anything more has happened." Did I want to tell him about another note, especially this note? Not on your life, but hadn't I promised him that I would let him know if anything further happened, and hadn't I already settled the debate about his right to know?

"I got another one," I blurted out.

"Another note? Oh, no."

"Yes."

"Implicating both of us?"

"That's right." I hoped he would let it go at that, but he didn't. "Could you read it to me?" he asked.

"Read it?" Sure, I could read his name, and I could read my name, but how could I tell him the impact was from a picture, not words, this time? I don't know how long I stood there like a dunce before I heard his voice pull me back.

"Are you all right?"

"Yeah."

"You don't sound like it. What does it say, Katie?" he insisted. "If you don't want to read the words, just paraphrase it for me. I really need to stay on top of this situation, you know."

"I understand. Well, the thing is, Mr. Grayson, I can't read this one. It's a . . . a picture with our names on it, and it's . . . well . . . really explicit."

After a lengthy silence, he said, "This doesn't work very well over the phone, does it? Would you mind if I came over?"

When he did, it was to the back door. "Hi," he greeted distractedly.

"Come on in," I said as it hit me how weird it felt to be inviting my second period teacher in. He had changed from his suit to jeans and a yellow golf shirt, which made him look younger and, I don't know, un-teacherly.

Would people believe this stuff about us if it got out? At that point, I almost wished the guy in the note had been Mr. Breen. No one would pay attention to it then. Instead, unbelievably, Timothy Grayson was following me into the kitchen.

"Why don't we sit down right here?" I motioned to the small table in the nook.

"Would you like some coffee or a soda?"

"Nothing right now, thanks."

"Okay." I sat down opposite him. "Mr. Grayson, I appreciate your coming over like this, but I'm not sure you really want to see this."

"You said it's explicit. In a sexual way? Look, Katie, I know this is an awkward topic. I'm no more comfortable with this than you are. But this seems to be escalating. We need to do something, and I need to know what I'm dealing with."

"I guess you're right," I said with a mixture of dread and resignation as I fished the note out of my pocket. It was folded several times, and I handed it to him that way.

As if in slow motion, he uncreased it, and that's when the knowledge that he was actually going to see it hit me full force. I thought I'd die to share something so personal with the living, breathing man across the table from me. I wanted nothing more than to snatch it out of his hands before he fully opened the page, but it was too late.

"Good grief!" he exploded as he stared at the figures labeled as us. He shook his head. Then he methodically refolded the page and lay it on the table between us. He looked from the note to me and must have seen something in my face. "Are you all right?"

"I'm so embarrassed."

"I understand. I'm sorry you had to see something this sensitive. Katie, let's focus away from the image and talk about the situation. How did you say you got this?"

"It arrived last night when no one was here. The woman who's staying with me while my parents are in Europe found it when she came in last night."

"She saw this?"

"No, luckily it was in an envelope."

"I'm glad to hear that. Well, we have to do something.

This has gone far enough."

He ran this fingers through his hair in that gesture I'd seen in his office.

"But what?" I asked. "I've spent hours trying to figure out who and why."

"And what have you come up with?"

"That's the thing, Mr. Grayson. Nothing. I can't think of anyone I know who would do this to me."

"Same here," he said. "Maybe if we consider the possibilities, no matter how remote, we'll hit upon something."

"It's worth a try, but where do we start?"

"Since you are the recipient of the note, let's begin with your friends and acquaintances," he suggested. It reminded me a little of my conversation with Rachel when she'd asked if I had any enemies—Just the facts, ma'am—but this was a whole lot more serious. I still didn't think it was one of my friends, but then again, lowed it to Mr. Grayson to cooperate, and maybe he and I would come up with something that Rachel and I had missed.

"Okay," I said. "I have a best friend who goes back to pre-school. Most of my other current friendships started around seventh grade, except for Rachel. She just moved here from Seattle at the beginning of the school year. But, Mr. Grayson, I can't imagine anyone of them wanting to do something cruel like this to me, or to you, for that matter."

"For argument's sake, though, let's just go down the list."

"I don't really want to name names."

"I can understand that, Katie, and I admire your loyalty, but the names may be crucial. There may be one that rings a bell for me."

"I see your point." I told him, first, about Maren and Laura.

"They sound like the Bobbsey Twins."

"The who?"

"Never mind. I just meant that they do a lot together. They are both in my class, though, so let's not rule them out. Tell me about the old friend."

"That's Elena. Elena Banning."

"Why do I detect some hesitation when you mention Elena?" he asked.

"Maybe because I don't know how to describe what's going on between us, or really understand it myself. It's complicated."

"I'm listening."

I explained how her parents' separation had closed her off, even to me, and how I had tried so hard to get through to her, but couldn't. "Nothing works," I said, "but I know she's not the one."

"How can you be so sure? Katie, look at the facts here. She sounds very fragile emotionally right now, and people, even nice people, do odd, sometimes hurtful, things when they are distressed. And Elena's also in one of my classes. I respect your instincts here, but maybe you shouldn't rule her out entirely, either."

It's not Elena, something inside me insisted. "Okay," I said to appease him.

"And how much do you know about Rachel?"

"Not a whole lot, but I haven't known her long enough for there to be any grudges or bad feelings. We've never even argued. Besides, she's been so supportive of me ever since this note

"I suppose Sharon Fleming could hold a grudge."

"How so?" he asked, and I told him about the way she'd reacted when I had beaten her out for the only vacant alto chair at choir try-outs.

"She's not in any of my classes, though."

He paused momentarily. "What about guys? I'm not trying to intrude here, you know, but is there anyone you dropped? Someone who's jealous? Anyone new to you around the time this started? Anyone at all you can think of?"

"Well, there's Todd Glanders, I suppose."

"What about Todd Glanders? He's in my junior lit class."

"It's just that old, old story. He wouldn't take no for an answer, but it got nasty."

"And?" he prompted.

"We were in a swimming pool and he pinned me to the side of it. Nothing I said helped. When he wouldn't let me go for the longest time, I finally slapped him really hard. He threatened me. He said, 'You'll be sorry for this.' But that was last summer, Mr. Grayson. He hasn't paid any attention to me at all since then."

"Okay, but a threat is a threat. Let's keep Todd as a possibility. What about a current boyfriend?"

I blushed.

"Paul Dumont," I said.

"He's also in junior lit."

"But it wouldn't be him."

"Um. Why not?"

Because we sing so beautifully together, Mr. Grayson, I wanted to tell him. But I knew that was a stupid reason. *Because I'm halfway in love with Paul.* No, that didn't carry any weight, either.

"He's just very nice," I said lamely.

"All right. I can see the stars in your eyes. Just don't let them blind you." He paused for a moment, and I noticed him scrutinizing me.

"What?" I asked.

"There is another possibility. Katie, do you remember

that news coverage last spring about the girl in another part of Oregon who said she was attacked in the school restroom?"

"Yeah." What was he getting at? The girl had said she was raped. She came from a good family and was an honors student who had never been in trouble at school, so everyone believed her. Of course there had been an investigation, though, and when the authorities started grilling her and her story had fallen apart, she finally confessed that she had made it all up.

"What are you getting at?" I asked. "Do you remember the outcome?"

"Just that she made the whole thing up. Why someone would do something like that is beyond me."

"We can't know the specifics," he said with a shrug. "Maybe her home life wasn't stable. Maybe she was in some kind of personal crisis. Or maybe she just craved attention. People do act out and do strange things, Katie, and it's because the why of something can be difficult for the stable mind to plumb that we've been focusing more upon the who behind this note situation."

He looked at me again with that probing look. Then he reached to the middle of the table and picked up the folded piece of paper for a moment before he set it back down and spoke again.

"Things like this have been known to happen when a young woman becomes infatuated with a teacher. Katie, if that's happening here, we can deal with it, but let's do it before this explodes and embarrasses us both on a wider scale."

All of a sudden, what he was saying hit me like a Mack truck, and my feelings fragmented into surprise, deep embarrassment, and indignation.

"You think I . . ."

"No, no, Katie, I don't think anything. We're just

covering the possibilities here. Remember?"

"Yeah. Well, Mr. Grayson, I can tell you right now that I'd never do anything like this. Not to you. Not to myself."

When I looked at that vile paper lying between us and thought of the other two suggestive notes, I felt totally sick to be considered as the source of such trash. Possibilities? Infatuations? Wasn't an accusation an accusation? Where was he coming off, anyway? It worked two ways. Sure, I'd been getting the stupid things, but his name was on them just as boldly as mine. When I spoke again, it was with a lot of emotion.

"I hate to bring this up, but what about you? We've been talking about my friends and people who might hold grudges against me, but what about you, Mr. Grayson? Your name is on there, too," I said as I stabbed a finger on top of the note.

He almost smiled.

"Fair enough. By nature, a teacher does attract a certain number of complaints . . . perhaps even some grudges. There's the grade a student thinks isn't high enough, the test that's allegedly not fair, the discipline that's necessary but not well-received."

When he seemed to look inward, I asked, "Were you thinking of something in particular?"

"Actually, yes. I'd almost forgotten. Now that I think of it, it's odd that you mentioned Sharon Fleming, because when I coached women's tennis and she was on the team, I had to suspend her. She took the discipline very poorly."

"I didn't know about that."

"Sharon was one of my best players, but she continually skipped practice and showed up late. It was disruptive to the team."

"I guess that gives her a reason to dislike both of us."

"She may, but then again, as you said about Todd

Glanders, why wait until now?

The suspension happened last April. Still, she's on both our lists. Let's not drop Sharon too fast."

"She does sound like a good candidate. Well, what else? What about your friends?" I asked.

"My friends? Most of them are teachers, Katie, and one thing I feel certain of is that no teacher would ever do anything like this to another teacher. Besides, I'm on cordial terms with the faculty. Most of the other people I know are students and neighbors, or they fall into the acquaintance category. This is only my second year at Oak Meadow, so I don't have the local contacts a longtime resident would."

"Well, I don't know how to ask this, but what about . . ."

"Ladies?"

I nodded, glad that he had filled in the word. Asking a teacher about his personal life was unreal.

"There's no one special. I didn't break anyone's heart, if that's what you are wondering. In fact," he volunteered with a mirthless little laugh, "The last woman I dated dropped me and is now engaged to someone else, so I'm drawing a blank there."

"Somewhere there has to be something."

When he spoke again, he didn't say anything I had anticipated. "You know, I think I would like that cup of coffee now."

"Sure," I told him as I got up to pour us each a mug. He stood up, stretched, and discreetly asked me where the bathroom was. Cognac, who had been fast asleep in her basket, growled.

When we finally sat back down, we sipped the hot liquid quietly for a few moments. Only Cognac relaxed. The note lay between us on the table like a live coal. It was impossible not to keep glancing at it, and I think we both got lost in our thoughts as we slowly drank our coffee. When I looked up, he was watching me.

"You don't think this will leak out, do you?" I asked. "I mean, would people believe this?"

He took a deep swig of coffee and carefully set the mug down before he answered, "They might."

They might? No, he was supposed to reassure me! He was supposed to tell me that no one would believe for long that cool Mr. Grayson would have a "thing" with girl-next-door Katie Krieg. I realized how badly I'd wanted him to say he was here just for minor damage control.

"You look flabbergasted, Katie. Is that so hard to believe? Don't sell yourself short. You exude just the kind of attractive innocence that would make this especially ugly if it were to come out."

My eyes strayed again to the little square of paper in the center of the table. Even though I couldn't see the pasted-on figures with my eyes, they had been so emblazoned on my brain, along with our names, that I saw them again anyway. He seemed to read my thoughts.

"Yes, there are people who would believe that of us."

I tried to sip my beverage, but my hands shook so much that I had to set the mug back down.

"I can't . . ."

He reached across the table then and touched my hand lightly.

"Katie, look at me." When I did, he asked, "What are you feeling right now?"

"Scared."

"So am I . . . and I'm not coming on to you when I say this, but it's imaginable, Katie. It's imaginable, and that's the danger of it. Believe me, I know how out-of-hand a situation can get."

"What do you mean?"

He shook his head as if to banish a bad memory. "One

of the reasons I haven't gone to the principal or anyone else about this is that something like this happened to me before."

"With notes and stuff? At Oak Meadow?"

"No, nothing with notes, and it wasn't at Oak Meadow. It happened my first year out of college, in Ohio. I couldn't get a position teaching English that first year, so I subbed. Subs, as you may know, can be put anywhere, and one of my spots turned out to be in wood shop."

"Wood shop?"

"Wood shop," he verified. "In my day, only boys took it, but now girls have that option in many schools. Jessica was bright, high-spirited and, sometimes, the class clown. Well, one day she started playing around with the table saw. I don't know if you've seen one of those, but they're nothing to fool around with. They have twelve-inch blades and revolve amazingly fast. They have to be extremely sharp to cut wood. Of course stringent safety precautions have to be taken when they are in use. Why, one of those blades could destroy an arm or sever a finger as easily as going through butter.

"And there was Jessica doing a damsel-in-distress parody with the turned-on saw. It was an extremely dangerous situation for her, Katie, but her attitude also had infected others, and the way they were goofing around near her made it dangerous for them as well. I told her three times to turn the saw off, but she continued showing off, and the situation quickly escalated to the point where I had to act immediately."

As Mr. Grayson seemed to be looking back, seeing the scene again, I, too, envisioned this Jessica person flitting around the dangerous machine.

"What happened?" I asked.

"I pushed her out of the way and reached for the switch to turn the saw off. She fell into a wall but was safe."

"You did the right thing."

"I thought so. I still do. But an embarrassed, maybe even humiliated, Jessica ran out of class. She ran straight home and told her parents that I had not only pushed he but touched her in an inappropriate place. Her parents rushed back to school and demanded that the principal take action against me. There was a full investigation. I didn't get any calls to substitute for the remainder of the year. In essence, I became an untouchable.

"That must have been terrible."

"It was. Even though I was exonerated at the hearing, thanks to the testimony of the other students who had witnessed Jessica's behavior and my push, the school district wouldn't hire me the following fall, and the only place I could teach that next year was in a small town on the other side of the state. I don't have anything against small towns, but I felt as though I were in exile. When I finally got this position here in Oregon, it was a fresh start.

"Katie, I love my work. I can't afford a scandal, especially not one of a sexual nature. I'm not trying to minimize what it would do to you if this leaks out, but for me the stakes are even higher. Why, something like this would probably destroy my whole career!"

And there were no witnesses this time. I felt powerless to say anything to help him. In the end, he began speaking again.

"It was bad enough with Jessica, but this is more complicated. The accusation is more volatile than a push or even a touch. Not only is the conduct alluded to in these notes the exploitation of a student by a teacher, but given your age, Katie, I'm being accused of something . . . criminal."

"Oh, Mr. Grayson!" was all I could say. I wanted to reassure him that I wasn't another Jessica, that I'd vouch for his integrity, but I realized at that moment just how sticky and complex this thing was. It wasn't just a case of our good word. In fact, to some people, our denial might even seem like guilt. No, it all came down to the horrible rumor mill, to innuendo, and to the awful human trait within the kind of person who wants to believe the worst in others.

"The rumor mill versus us," I said dully, "And it loves to get pumped up. That's why we're here this afternoon trying to get some perspective."

"Perspective . . ."

"What are you thinking?" he asked.

"When we were talking earlier, I wasn't thinking too much about the past as perspective."

"Is there something in yours?"

"Well, no, not really, but there's probably something I should tell you about myself. You see, even though this wouldn't be criminal for me, I can't afford a scandal, either. I know what it's like to be judged unfairly, and I have things in my past that I need to keep buried, just like you don't want the Jessica thing to come back to haunt you.

"I'm not trying to make a big mystery out of this," I said with a self-conscious little laugh.

"I know. Take your time." The way he didn't press me helped release the words. "I have this seizure disorder, Mr. Grayson. It's not grand mal or what most people think of, though. I had encephalitis, and almost from day one people didn't understand how it affected me. The illness changed something in my brain. It's the kind of thing that mimics emotional or psychological problems. At first, they put it down to tantrums. Then behavior problems. 'Snap out of it Katie. Why are you doing this, Katie?' And I didn't have any answers because I didn't know why. The worst thing is, I didn't even know what I'd done . . . at least not until I saw some evidence afterwards."

"Evidence?" he prompted, and something in me froze.

How much should I tell him? Wouldn't he just brand me an emotionally disturbed teenager, or worse? What was I getting myself into? I just couldn't stand to be judged unfairly still again.

"Katie, it's all right." The gentle assurance of his voice made me think of how he had bared his soul about Jessica and his teaching exile. It was just my turn now, and I had to hope he had an open mind.

"Like broken things," I said.

"Broken things? I'm really interested here, Katie. Could you give me an example?"

"I guess. Well, one time I was just doing something in the family room. I don't even remember what. But something happened. Again, I don't remember what. The next thing I knew was that I was . . . I was stomping on a wall picture and smashing its glass. It sounds crazy, I know."

"And you don't remember any of it?"

"No, only coming out of it, only the shame after it happened. And people not understanding."

"This finally came to a head, I take it."

"That's right. Finally something even more destructive happened. I was practically accused of being a juvenile delinquent. I mean, it got ugly. All through it, my mother insisted that I wasn't a bad person and that there had to be some physical explanation for my occasional burst of weird behavior. Finally, at her insistence, they ran tests. It was the EEG that showed I had brain damage. It's when the seizure disorder was discovered."

"And they didn't suspect it after your illness?"

"No."

"That sounds like an incredible oversight to me."

"I know. Anyway, we've sort of pieced things together. We now know that light effects, like pulsating strobes, set off something in my brain. It's like an overload. Back when

I stomped that picture, there may have been something intense on television. Who knows? Even today, even now that I'm on an anticonvulsant medication, I avoid certain kinds of lights. I don't really have any trouble if I do. "But, you know, it's there, lurking. I can't forget. And I remember how people treated me. I don't ever want to be thought of as Crazy Katie Krieg again, Mr. Grayson!"

"Of course you don't. Katie, do your friends know about your seizure disorder?"

"Very few. Most just think I have to avoid certain films and lights because they give me headaches. It's not something you go around advertising."

"You needn't be ashamed, either, Katie. You didn't ask to get sick or have brain damage, and it wasn't your fault that the medical community let you down by not diagnosing your seizure disorder much earlier."

"Yeah, I know all that on an intellectual level. It's just that if this note stuff did get out, I'm sure there are some who would suspect me, Mr. Grayson. But I can assure you, I'm taking my medication."

"There's been a lot of cutting and pasting going on here, Katie. If you were doing this, there would be some evidence, just as there was with the broken picture."

"I appreciate your saying that."

"Well, it's true."

"Anyway, now you know why the stakes are high for me, too," I said. "I do have an idea about handling this situation."

"Anything."

"Well, it goes back to what we were talking about earlier. You know, about why us, and what the connection between us is in this person's mind. Maybe the sender is feeding upon seeing us together at school. My idea is that maybe I should skip your class for a few days."

"To defuse the situation?"

"Yeah."

"That's not a bad suggestion. The only thing is, this person seems to have quite a mission, and I think your avoiding me in that context might just add fuel to the fire. But let me think about it."

"I'll do anything," I told him with feeling.

"I know, and I appreciate that. Have you told anyone else about the third note?"

"No. No one but the two of us know it's a picture."

"I think we should keep it that way, but I also think that in spite of what I've said about wanting to keep this to ourselves, we could be reaching the point of needing to share it with someone else. I worry, too, about your lack of support. When will you parents be home?"

"Not for another week."

"We may need someone else's input before then. I don't know who that would be."

"Me, either, except . . ."

"I'm up for any suggestions."

"I was thinking of Ms. Daniels. She used to be at my old school, in junior high, and she helped me a lot with a problem. Everything you say to her stays confidential."

"Tanisha Daniels? The counselor? She transferred to Oak Meadow this school year, didn't she?"

"That's right. Anyway, if we tell anyone, she might be the one."

"Okay, let's let that be our plan. Nothing has really changed, but we've talked this out about as far as we can today, I think. Katie, I appreciate your frankness."

"And I appreciate yours."

As we got up, Cognac came to life again.

"You let me know if anything more happens. And, Katie, be in class on Monday." As we reached the door and I stepped out with him to assure him I'd be in class, Cognac made such a beeline for Mr. Grayson's ankles that she toppled me. Fortunately, he reacted fast and kept me from falling off the porch.

It was a strange ending to an unreal afternoon.

Day 6
Sunday

I f had known how awful the day was going to get, I'm sure that I would have been thinking about other things the next morning in church. But I didn't know, and from my vantage point in the choir loft, my eyes gravitated toward Andrea Combs.

Was there any truth to what Maren had insinuated about Andrea and Paul the night before?

Her phone call had begun routinely enough with a list of movie possibilities we might see together. Actually, after such an emotional afternoon with Mr. Grayson, I felt so wrung out that I could take it or leave it. I knew for sure I had to forget it when Maren said how jazzed up she and Laura were about seeing part of the Star Wars trilogy.

"You know, I think I'll skip it," I said as I thought of all the special light effects. "Oh, that's right," Maren remembered. "Your headaches."

If only they knew . . .

Was I wrong to hide my seizure disorder from them? Wouldn't they have compassion? Or would knowing just make them uncomfortable around me? Compassion,

I realized, was a double-edged sword, since few things in life hurt as much as feeling the absence of it. I knew I was also afraid, afraid of not being liked, afraid of not being accepted because this person or that person just couldn't fathom the complexities of the human brain.

No, I wouldn't lie to anyone about it, but I wouldn't tell people I didn't have to, either. I let the headache excuse stand with Laura and Maren.

"We could see something else," Maren offered.

"That's sweet of you, but I think I'd rather just stay home tonight. You can tell me all about Star Wars."

"Well, if you're sure." When I didn't take her up on her offer, she changed the subject. "I thought you said that Paul was flying to Sacramento right after the memorial service."

"He was."

"That's odd."

"What do you mean?"

"I saw him at four-thirty having a burger at Giant. He was with Andrea Combs."

It couldn't have been Paul. He had been rushing to catch his flight even as Mr. Soderquist's service ended. And Andrea Combs? She was in Paul's class at Oak Meadow, but where did she fit in?

"They say we all have a look-alike," I joked to Maren.

Maren, though, insisted that she would know Paul Dumont anywhere, and I knew she really had seen Paul.

I thought of Mr. Grayson. Possibilities, he had said, think of the possibilities, no matter how remote. A shadow crossed my thoughts.

Could it be Paul doing this to me? Did he just want me to think he was going to be out of town? Had he been making things up all along, including his feelings for me? I had to admit that it was sort of odd that, out of the blue, he'd asked me out just around the time the note stuff had begun.

"I'm sure he just missed his plane," I rationalized. I didn't try to explain Andrea. Now, in church, the sunlight streaming through a stained-glass window turned her hair into a river of liquid gold. A biggish nose kept her from being beautiful, but she had a figure the guys liked.

Still, Andrea and Paul? Why take me out if he and Andrea were an item? When I remembered that magical evening with him, I just couldn't believe there was anything going on. He wasn't the note sender. He'd just missed his flight, and there must also be an explanation for the burger with the junior the guys talked about longingly.

As the minister got more deeply into his sermon, I just couldn't focus upon his words.

Why had Maren even gotten into the Giant hamburger issue? I mean, why tell me my new boyfriend hadn't caught his plane and, worse, that he was eating with another girl?

Come to think of it, hadn't Maren and Laura acted sort of weird toward me ever since they'd learned that Paul had asked me out? Were they jealous or something? Why try to spoil something good for me?

That kind of thinking was getting me nowhere. I tuned back into the sermon and made a resolution not to let my mind wander off again.

"This is my afternoon to visit Georgia," Mrs. Pemberton reminded me as we finished dinner after church.

"Oh, that's right." Her sister had recently moved to a retirement community, and I should have remembered from last week that Mrs. Pemberton spent Sundays with her. "Why don't you just go ahead? I'll clean up."

"You may not want to when you see the sink full of pots," she laughed.

"I don't mind at all," I assured her after complimenting her again on her veal piccata. She was a terrific cook, which always surprised me, since I knew she had danced on Broadway many years ago.

"Do you have something to do this afternoon?"

"Do I? Scads and scads of homework."

"Okay, then. There's leftover chicken in the fridge. I'll be back in time for that good television movie tonight."

"Good. I'm looking forward to it, too. Have a nice visit with your sister."

"Thank you, dear."

I was just finishing in the kitchen when Rachel called. "Well?" I asked. "How did it go?"

"In a word, super," she said breathlessly. "Jason's really cool. And I did buy that green sweater you told me about. Anyway . . ."

She told me about the movie, the Chinese food, and their ride home.

"He stopped along the river. I thought he was going to be another one of those guys. You know . . ."

I'd known Jason Porter since kindergarten and knew he was one nice guy, but then again, how well did I know the current Jason? For Rachel's sake I hoped he hadn't turned out to be the kind who thought "looking at the river" with a girl was an invitation.

"And was he that way?" I asked.

"Not at all. It was funny, really, because when we stopped and looked out at the water, he told me all about the big flood of '96. I mean, it wasn't some kind of line, either."

"Yeah, he's always been a pretty okay guy."

"He's all that! Say, what have you heard from Paul?"

"Actually, nothing. It's only been a day, Rachel, but already I miss him so. I'm not sure when he'll be back from

California." I didn't tell her about the Andrea Combs thing.

"And what's been happening otherwise?"

Her question made me realize just how much had been happening: a new note, Mr. Grayson's visit the afternoon before, and the way this was wearing me down. I wasn't trying to keep anything from Rachel in particular, but I became aware just then that something in me had changed. Maybe a little of the childlike innocence had disappeared as, in its place, I felt a new kind of responsibility. Some of the issues Mr. Grayson and I had talked about were very personal. The fact that he had even come over was sensitive. And I knew that he counted on my discretion. I wasn't free to tell Rachel some things.

"Katie?"

"I'm still here," I said.

"Well, did you get another note or something?" I guessed I could reveal that much.

"Yeah, I did."

"Oh, no. What did it say this time?"

"Just let me say it was lewd, Rachel."

"Well, what are you going to do? Are you going back to Mr. Grayson?"

"Probably. Right now, I'm just trying to push it all into the back of my mind. I've got a pile of homework, including that essay, which I haven't even begun."

"So you have no new leads?"

"Not really."

"You don't seem to want to talk about it," she said.

"I know."

"Yeah, well, I hope you get to the bottom of it soon."

"Thanks." We were about talked out and hung up soon after that.

I did try to push the situation into the back of my mind that afternoon. I got geometry out of the way and started thinking about the persuasive letter for Mr. Grayson's class.

On my PC, I wrote a few lines on world population. Then as my focus changed entirely, I turned away from the computer, pulled out pen and paper, and began writing:

Dear Elena,

It's been one rough week, and it's funny, but in good times or bad, it remains you to whom I want to turn. Some people might put it down to habit, but it isn't really that. No, it boils down to two individuals having "clicked" and, over time, made a mutual decision, through respect and caring, to trust, confide in, and be there for each other.

The start of the letter wasn't quite right, but it felt good to be doing something to at least try to salvage the friendship that meant so much to me. I wanted Elena to read my feelings in my own writing. And a printed version would be a perfect way to meet Mr. Grayson's assignment.

But could I persuade Elena?

I picked up my pen again:

I am being harassed, Elena, and the whole, bizarre situation has plunged me straight into a nightmare. They are notes by an anonymous someone—notes that accuse me of doing something very wrong with a nice man whose reputation could be ruined if this leaks out. What makes it so unspeakable is that the man happens to be my teacher.

I feel violated just to think that someone imagines something like this.

Elena, sometimes I'm so enraged by the nameless accusations that I feel like smashing something. I also feel embarrassed because the teacher knows. And I feel scared that it's going to get out and blow up in our faces. You, of all

people, know how sensitive I am to being judged
unfairly.

It's bad enough to fear being called "Crazy
Katie" again, but it's downright creepy to go to
school, see scores of people, many of whom I
consider friends, and wonder if the note sender
is one of them.

Still as horrible as my situation is, it is
situational and, I try to keep in mind, temporary.
That doesn't make it easy to handle.

For you, though, the very fabric of life has
been torn.

Did I like the fabric analogy? I wasn't sure and put
down my pen. What was it like for Elena? Maybe her life
seemed as smashed to smithereens as that glass had been
on the picture I had stomped. How do we know another's
turmoil? Was I presumptuous to, as Elena herself had put it,
butt in, or was it the compassionate thing to do?

Compassion: I focused upon that word, and I thought
again about my talk with Elena that day in her driveway.

You told me that I can't know what you
are going through. That's certainly true. But
we are friends, Elena, and on a very special
level where understanding just happens and
acceptance is unconditional, I can understand,
and I do sympathize with your situation and
support you one hundred percent.

Suddenly inspired, I wrote about instances from our
shared past, wrote about love, wrote about the essence of
friendship. And in the end, I returned to that fabric of life
analogy that I had almost thrown out. I finished with the
simple plea:

Please let me help you reweave it.

It was done. I had some time to rethink certain passages and to hone it on my PC for the assignment, but the longhand version for Elena was essentially done. Maybe it would help, and maybe it wouldn't, but at least I hadn't given up on her.

It was when I went to get an envelope from my all-purpose drawer that I got the shock of my life.

It was something very foreign and totally unexpected . . . something that didn't belong in the drawer.

What is this? something inside me screamed. Even though my eyes registered what they were seeing, my brain denied it and froze. I don't know how much time passed before I reached into my drawer with icy fingers.

It couldn't be, could it?

I pulled out the magazine. Two alphabet letters from its masthead were missing, hacked out with scissors, and from the color of those remaining, I knew that one of them was a big, hot pink "G" that had gone onto the third note: the "G" in the "Grayson" pasted over that awful picture.

"This has to be a nightmare," I said out loud.

I finally leafed through the rest of the magazine and found other pages with letters missing here and there that matched those on the notes.

There was even some plain typewriter paper tucked between the pages of the magazine, all ready to go, and a glue stick that wasn't mine. I picked it up. I'd never liked the sticks and didn't use them.

I dropped it like a hot potato as the realization of what I'd found sank in.

This was terrible! Someone had planted this stuff in my room. The notes had been bad enough, but to think that someone had sneaked into my own private sanctuary . . . .

Was this person getting dangerous? Should I call the police? But even as I wondered, I knew I shouldn't—not without talking to Mr. Grayson about it first—because then everything would really be out in the open.

As the initial shock of discovery wore off, I even thought of a positive side to this.

Evidence: This was hard, tangible evidence, and evidence might mean clues to help us narrow the possibilities.

I was about to call Mr. Grayson when the memory of his words jarred me with heart-stopping dread: "There's been a lot of cutting and pasting going on here, Katie. If you were doing it, there would be some evidence, just as there was with the broken picture."

Evidence . . .

Oh, my God!

Could I . . .

"Consider the possibilities, no matter how remote," he had advised.

Could I cross my heart and hope to die that I hadn't done this myself?

Okay, calm down, Katie. It's just a possibility, like all the others.

Wouldn't I know if had done this? Could someone put notes together and plant them without remembering?

I sucked in my breath. I had done things—terrible things—without knowing, without remembering. There had been no logic to any of it. No, it had been just crummy electrical charges not working right in my brain. Okay, these were notes. Were notes destructive like, say, a broken picture? I suppose they were. They destroyed peace of mind, that's for sure. Still, wouldn't I know?

Yet who else would be doing this? Mr. Grayson and I hadn't come up with any answers. He'd talked about infatuations. Did I have some subconscious feelings for him?

Was this my way of getting him to notice me, to maybe even think of me as more than just another student?

It didn't make much sense, but then again, it made no sense at all that anyone else would be after both him and me.

I was doing it! How could I ever live down the shame? A broken picture, lamps in the snow—those things were one type of thing. But Mr. Grayson was a human being. He'd been so nice about this whole thing, and especially as I remembered his experience in Ohio, I couldn't stand the thought that maybe I was doing this new awful thing to him. He'd had his share. How could I ever face him?

At least it hadn't gotten out. Rachel knew some of it. I'd told Paul I was being harassed. And of course Mr. Grayson knew. But that was only a few people. I couldn't let it spread, not even to one extra person.

And that led me to recall my suggestion of telling Ms. Daniels. Why had I said that? Had Mr. Grayson and I settled on telling her for sure? I couldn't even remember.

What if the principal and all my other teachers found out? What if my friends all dropped me? What if they sent me away somewhere as incorrigible . . . or worse: Crazy Katie.

No, I couldn't afford even one more person knowing. Not if I were doing it! Like a zombie, I reached for the phone. Dialing his number brought me back to life again, and I listened to each painful ring.

"Hello." I cringed at the sound of Mr. Grayson's voice. What if he guessed?

How would I ever explain? Act normal.

"Hi, it's Katie. I hope you don't mind my calling."

"Of course not, but I hope this doesn't mean that you've received another one."

"No, I haven't. It's just that I've rethought telling Ms.

Daniels or anyone. Can we hold off on that?"

"We hadn't really decided to tell her," he reminded me. "Katie, what's going on?" Should I tell him anything? He did have the right to be kept up-to-date on this, but then again, telling him anything seemed premature. I wasn't ready, anyway, to face the shame. I'd just die if he knew or even suspected.

But I had to say something. I'd called him.

"Well," I said, "I have a suspect."

"Good. Who is it you suspect? Anyone on our list?"

"I'm not ready to name the person."

"You' re not trying to play detective, are you? You know, this person has just sent notes so far, but we don't know what is going on in his or her mind, either. We can't be sure this person isn't potentially dangerous, or wouldn't be if confronted. So, please don't do anything rash."

"I won't," I promised.

"All right. We will reassess this tomorrow. Remember, Katie, it's honorable to want to protect a friend, but sometimes friends need help that we can't give them ourselves. There's no dishonor in getting that help for another person."

I wondered which of my friends he thought I suspected. ''I'll remember that. Thanks."

"We'll work this out," he said energetically.

"I know."

I felt totally sick as I hung up the phone.

Day 7
Monday

"Hi," I said. As usual, Mrs. Stellema was at her desk scanning the computer. "Oh, hello, Katie." She smiled. Then, a bit puzzled, the receptionist checked the appointment book.

"I know I'm not in the book, but is Dr. Emry in? It won't take long. It's just that it's sort of important." I probably should have called first, but I had the idea that he would be more likely to see me if I were already in the office. When Mrs. Stellema frowned, though, I think I knew the bad news before she said it.

"Gee, I'm sorry. He's at a convention in Chicago."

Oh great! My parents were out of the country, my best friend might just as well be on the moon, and now my doctor wasn't even available.

"Oh. Well . . ."

She must have caught the disappointment in my voice. Maybe it had even been tinged with the desperation I felt. Whatever, Mrs. Stellema walked from her office into the waiting room and motioned for me to sit down. Then she sat beside me on the leather couch.

"Are you having a problem? Dr. Emry will be back the day after tomorrow, but if it's something urgent, he is referring his patients to Dr. Tanaka. I could try to squeeze you in if it's an emergency."

"Thanks. Um, it's not the kind of emergency you probably mean. It's just that I need some advice."

"Is there any way I can help?"

"Probably not."

"Well, why don't you try me? I can try with anything but actual medical matters." Whether or not this was a "medical matter" was the point. In fact, the answer was crucial. If it was a medical matter—at least one that concerned me—I was doing this awful thing. If not, then somebody else was. It was just all so complicated that suddenly the whole thing got to me, and I started to cry.

Mrs. Stellema reached for the box of tissues on the magazine table and held it out. "Here."

"Thanks," I sputtered.

"Look, I'm going to squeeze you in."

I looked at her and nodded. I had no way of knowing if Dr. Tanaka could be of any help, but the prospect of doing anything at all made me feel a little better, and I gave the receptionist a weak smile.

I tried to blank things out as she returned to her desk and I waited, but all the magazines on the table just made me think again of the jolt of finding that terrible cut-up one in my drawer.

It really made me wish that my own doctor was here. Dr. Emry was always friendly, and yet he had a starched look and pewter-colored hair that made him look like somebody who knew things other people did not. And, of course, he did. In fact, I'm sure we would have caught my seizure disorder much earlier if he had been my doctor from the time I had encephalitis.

Dr. Tanaka was a lot younger. I'd seen him in the offices they shared, but I didn't really know him. When he finally called me in, I only hoped he had some of Dr. Emry's wisdom.

"I appreciate your seeing me on such short notice," I said as he ushered me in. He smiled and took the chair behind an oversize desk. Then he motioned me to the one on the other side.

"I'm glad I have a spot of time," he began. Mrs. Stellema told me that you have been Dr. Emry's patient for many years."

"For about six years."

"What brings you in between your regular visits?"

"Well, it's complicated, but what I need to know, Dr. Tanaka, is if somebody can be sending notes to herself without even knowing it."

By the way he looked at me, I could tell he knew that I was talking about myself, and I felt my face go crimson. Still, as awkward as the situation was, I needed an answer and I needed it as soon as I could get it.

"I can't tell you if you are or not. I don't have the knowledge of your history that your regular doctor does. Generally speaking—and one does have to beware of generalizations in medicine—it is possible that someone can be in a fugue state and not remember what's happened."

"A fugue state?"

"Blacking out."

Oh no! Wasn't blacking out what happened when I saw something like a strobe light and "woke up" to find that I had just stomped on a picture and broken the glass? So it was me! What was I going to do? I'd never be able to face Mr. Grayson again . . . or even live with myself

Dr. Tanaka must have seen my shock.

"I said possible, Katie, not probable. It's normal to be concerned, but you also need to take care not to indict yourself until you have all the facts and incontrovertible proof"

I somehow knew he meant medical proof, not some notes and a butchered magazine, so I didn't get into the nature of them. He was a neurologist, not a psychiatrist, after all.

"How much medication are you taking currently?" he asked. "Three hundred milligrams a day."

"Have you skipped any doses?"

"No. I'm really careful."

"And I see from your chart that you had a blood-level test recently." I nodded.

"Everything looks fine here. Katie, the best thing you can do for yourself is not to panic. Try to put the notes out of your mind for now, if you can, and I'll ask Mrs. Stellema to make an appointment for you with Dr. Emry at the earliest possible time."

He glanced at his watch. He must have a patient coming.

"Okay. Thanks, Dr. Tanaka."

"Remember, it's possible, not probable. I'm sorry I couldn't help more. If you need someone to talk to before Dr. Emry returns, I can give you a couple of names."

"Thank you. I think I'll just wait for him."

"That would be my advice. You'll be all right now?"

"Don't worry. If I need someone, there's a counselor at school." That seemed to reassure him, and the visit was over.

I hadn't talked to the doctor for more than ten minutes, but with the time I'd spent waiting to see him, plus the bus trip from his office to school, second period was just getting over by the time I arrived.

Of course during third period my mind kept straying to the situation. Possible, not probable, I kept reminding myself, and it helped a little. Still, possible was possible, and I knew I would feel a whole lot more reassured once I had seen my own doctor. For the time being, I would take Dr. Tanaka's advice to try not to indict myself

But if I wasn't doing this, it went back to the fact that someone else was, which meant that that person had broken into my house—my bedroom—to plant evidence. The idea was so creepy I shivered.

Concentrate on class, I told myself even as a mental list of who had had the opportunity to get into my room began forming in my mind. I tried to push it away. As much as I needed to get to the bottom of this, I couldn't afford to be in outer space, either, and have people go around asking, "What's the matter with Katie?"

Miraculously, I was focused when my geometry teacher asked me if I knew what a dodecahedron was.

After class, Rachel caught up with me. "Where were you?" she asked.

Trying to exonerate myself, I thought. What would Rachel's reaction be if she thought I suspected myself in this whole sorry mess? I was so frazzled just from concentrating so hard to stay focused in school that I couldn't think of anything to tell Rachel but the truth.

"I had a doctor's appointment," I said. "Are you sick?"

"No, I just have to go now and then. You know, about that thing I told you about."

"Oh, yeah. Well, Grayson just about had a meltdown. I mean, I could tell he was upset when he saw your chair vacant, Katie. What's going on?"

"The same old thing," I hedged. "So, what's happening there?"

"Nothing new today."

She gave me a searching look. "Well, if you don't want to share it with me . . ."

"No, Rachel. No note today . . . so far. Cross your fingers for me."

"I just get this feeling—you suspect someone, don't you?"

I didn't feel like going down any lists with Rachel or anyone else. Mr. Grayson and I had done that almost until we were blue in the face, and where had it gotten us? The drawer stuff was even more complicated. Still, Rachel meant well, and I didn't want to alienate her after she'd been so supportive in this.

"Yeah, sort of. Look Rachel, I'm sorry if I seem weird. I'm just sorting out a whole lot of stuff here."

Then out of the blue she named a name.

"You think it's Elena, don't you? Well, I think so, too."

Elena? Was she on that new suspect list that had been starting to materialize in geometry? In all honesty, I guess she had to be on it, she had a key to my house, and better than anyone else, she knew my room. Even so, it made me sick to hear my oldest friend's name as a suspect.

"What are you talking about? Why do you think it's Elena?" She'd better have a good answer.

"Well, don't get huffy. She's just acting weird, Katie. I mean, look at the way she avoids you like the plague and spends so much time brooding in a corner by herself. If you ask me, she's one sick cookie."

"Oh, come on, Rachel, that doesn't mean she's sending me notes."

"There! You're doing it again."

"Doing what?" I asked.

"Getting all defensive."

"Look, I appreciate your concern, Rachel. I just don't

think it's Elena. Maybe we should just let it drop."

"Okay, but I think you should keep her in mind."

"I'll do that," I said. Then I moved on.

At lunch, the conversation with Laura and Maren began almost the same way as it had with Rachel. As far as those two were concerned, I wasn't even sure I wanted to sit with them, not after Maren's strange insinuation about Paul and Andrea Combs, but they had saved me a seat, as usual, and called me over.

"I didn't see you earlier," Laura commented as I sat down. When I explained that I had had an appointment, they exchanged looks. What was going on with them?

"How are things going with Paul? Did he call?" Maren asked.

"What do you mean?"

"You know, after he got back," Maren clarified.

"He might have," I said. I'd been so zombied out last night from my discovery that I didn't even know. When I explained to my friends that I'd had a headache and unplugged my phone, this time the headache was not just an excuse. By the time I had thought back over how strange my behavior had sometimes been before we knew about the seizure thing, I did have a splitting head.

Right there in the lunchroom, my panic started to spiral all over again as guilt and shame over my past lapses moved back over me like black clouds. I'd done such bizarre things without remembering!

"Oh, there he is now," Laura informed me.

"Huh?"

"Earth to Katie," Maren said. "Paul"

"Oh," I said as my heart sank. If he was in the room, why hadn't he come over and said something to me?

"Look who he's with," Maren said. "Yeah, just look at them," Laura added.

I followed their eyes. Paul and Andrea were sitting very close, all caught up in something I couldn't see. Were they sharing a magazine or something? He said something to her, and she laughed with a toss of that super-long hair. Paul and I were hardly going together, and yet . . . and yet we'd made some kind of special connection. Or so I'd thought.

Then again, how well did I really know him? Was he a suspect, after all? Had he had the opportunity to slip that magazine into my drawer? *To be honest, he probably had,* I thought with a sinking feeling as I remembered how I'd shown him some old sheet music by the piano in the upstairs study before the concert. My room was just one door down, and hadn't I left him upstairs alone for a minute while I'd taken care of Cognac?

"Katie?" I heard Maren saying through my fog of doubt.

"I don't have an explanation for Andrea. I don't really want to talk about it." Why were they rubbing it in?

Laura and Maren: Were they on the mental list, too? I guessed they had to be, since Mrs. Pemberton had left the door unlocked for a couple of hours. She had apologized profusely for the oversight, but since nothing seemed to be missing from the house, it seemed to have been nothing. But what if something had been added, not taken?

No, I couldn't rule them out, either.

Rachel'd been in my room. Why, even Mr. Grayson could have planted the magazine, I realized. He'd gone to the bathroom while I poured our coffee. Suspects began to whirl around and around, until I felt nauseated.

"I don't feel so hot," I said to Maren and Laura. "I think I'm going to skip lunch." They gave me such sympathetic looks, like my relationship with Paul had been some pipe dream, that I felt even worse.

I was on my way to the restroom when as I left the cafeteria, Paul caught up with me.

"Hi," he said. "I tried calling when I got back last night."

"Did you?"

"Well, sure. Hey, did I do something wrong?"

The "something wrong" sidled up to us just then. With a toss of that hair, she greeted me. Then she looked me up and down sort of cattily and turned her attention back to Paul.

"Hello, Andrea." I kept the million questions I had to myself

"I'll see you later," she said, dripping honey, to Paul. I thought I'd puke. As Paul watched her walk to the other side of the room, he said, "Oh. You think . . ."

"I don't think anything. Besides, there's nothing between us."

"There isn't? I thought there was something sweet and special. Something to explore at greater length."

Boy, was he giving me mixed signals!

"I thought so, too." I looked down at my shoe, trying to hide the tears pooling in the comers of my eyes, and realized that I was afraid of being vulnerable. "Sweet and special . . . something to explore . . . ." Did he mean it the way I thought he had, or were they just words? If we had something special, why had he ignored me earlier and been head-to-head with Andrea Combs? Even my friends were implying that something was going on between them.

Well, I wasn't going to ask. I didn't own the guy.

"Hey," he said.

"What?"

"Katie, there's nothing romantic between Andrea and me. We are debate partners, and we were sitting over there working out our strategy."

I remembered their laughter. "Yeah, sure."

"We decided to inject a little humor into our argument, and I can see how it must have looked. But it's school stuff. That's all. Really."

"Really? Well . . ." The thought of Saturday stopped my thoughts in their tracks.

"Well?"

"Were you talking about the debate on Saturday, too? Some of my friends saw you two at Giant."

"Andrea's a neighbor." He explained how he had missed his ride to the airport after the memorial service and that the only other available flight wasn't until early evening. "In fact, her brother offered to drive me. I was surprised when she showed up instead."

"And you stopped for a burger on your way." I felt sort of sheepish. "Exactly. Forgive me?"

"There's nothing to forgive. Forgive me for overreacting."

"Does it have anything to do with what you told me about Friday?" he asked. "Yes. The situation has gotten a lot more complicated. I feel like biting people's heads off half the time."

"I can't blame you. We'll talk more about it. I plan to be seeing a lot of you, Katie Krieg, if that's all right with you."

"It's more than all right, Paul," I said as something heavy lifted from my spirit. I'd be free of this note situation soon, free to concentrate upon Paul and school and just things again.

"Good," he replied as lunch period ended.

I carried his smile with me as I left the room.

As I walked to my first class after lunch, I passed Mr. Grayson's classroom. Why did he have to be standing in the doorway? Well, maybe at least I could get by him without more than a nod. I just couldn't tell him that I suspected myself.

No such luck.

"Katie!" he called. Of course I stopped. "Are you all right? I missed seeing you in class this morning."

All right? No, I wasn't all right. When I wasn't suspicious of every friend I had, I zeroed in on myself like a teeter-totter it went, them, me, them, me.

"I'm fine," I said in a major understatement, but I must not have been very good at masking my emotions.

"Look, this isn't the time or place to talk. I'd like to see you in my office after your last class."

What could I say? I told him I'd be there.

The afternoon was weird as my emotions wavered between relief about Paul and dread over the prospect of being grilled by my teacher.

Mr. Grayson's door was open when I arrived, so he saw me.

"Come in, Katie." As I did, he got up from behind his desk, pushed the door almost closed, and then sat on the edge of the desk, close to my chair. He looked sort of impatient.

"I got here as quickly as I could," I said.

"You aren't late. Katie, I thought when we talked on Saturday, we decided how important it was that you be in class today. Especially after yesterday's brief phone conversation, I was concerned when you didn't show up. Is everything all right?"

"I didn't mean to worry you. I had every intention of being there."

"Then why weren't you?" His question was both gentle and insistent, inviting honesty.

"I had an appointment."

"One that you had forgotten?"

"Well . . . no . . . not really. In fact, it wasn't even a true appointment," I said, thinking about how I'd just walked, unscheduled, into Dr. Emry's office.

I knew that Mr. Grayson was waiting for more, but my mind just sort of shut down. He was sitting about two feet away, so alive and vital, with a future before him. How could I tell him how freaked I'd been to suddenly suspect myself? He had already been scorched by the Jessica fiasco. How could I reveal that I could be the one burning him now? Worse, would I end up being the one to send his career up on the flames of doubt and suspicion?

His voice cut through my thoughts. "You're very tense. What's happened?"

Possible, not probable, I reminded myself, and Dr. Tanaka's words gave me a surge of courage.

"I . . . I went to my doctor's this morning. Something did happen yesterday. It was so terrible, so unexpected, that it made me think of a new suspect, and the thought just totally freaked me out."

"Okay, but I don't see what that had to do with your going to—" He interrupted his own sentence, and it was as if I could see the gears mesh in his mind as he added,

"Oh . . ."

Our eyes met then, and it was as if his looked right into my soul. He knew. "This new suspect," he said.

"Me."

"Tell me about it."

And I did, from finding the magazine in my room through the consultation with Dr. Emry's fill-in.

"So, this Dr. Tanaka thinks it's very unlikely that you are doing this."

"Yes, but . . ."

". . . you aren't totally convinced," he finished for me.

"I try to be, but I'll feel a lot better once I've talked to my regular doctor."

"That's understandable."

"Mr. Grayson, I couldn't stand it if it were me!"

"I don't think it's you, but let's say it did turn out that way."

"But it . . ."

No 'buts', Katie. It would be a terrible blow to you, yet you'd get through it, find out why, and build your life from there. Dr. Emry's the best, I've heard. You'd have his support. You'd have your parents', I'm sure. And you'd have mine."

"I wouldn't want anybody making excuses for me because I have a seizure disorder."

"Not excuses, Katie, compassion. We'd have compassion."

"I don't see how you could. I'd never live it down."

"I could," he said quietly, "because I know you. I know you as my student. I know you from what we've talked about since this situation began. And I know it is taking courage for you to be honest with me now.

"But as I said, I don't think it's you, and that leaves us with another, very unsettling problem."

"A break-in," I filled in.

"Yes. You know, I think we need to share this with someone else."

"Tell someone? What if it is me? Can't we at least wait until I talk to Dr. Emry?" He thought it over and scratched his chin before answering. "I suppose so, but if we wait, you are going to have to be more careful than usual. Lock your doors at all times. Don't go out alone at night, even to walk your dog. We can't know what's going on in this person's mind."

"Do you think I'm in danger, then?"

"If I thought so, we wouldn't wait. But it doesn't hurt to take precautions. Now, who had the opportunity to plant that magazine?"

I ran down my list.

"So, it could be anyone," he said after I'd told him the door had been unlocked.

"That's right."

"And you have had no new notes, pictures . . . anything?"

"No, not since I discovered that magazine."

"That could be a good sign."

"Could it be? Do you think this has gone as far as it will?"

He bit his lip. "The truth? No, I don't, but I hope with every fiber of my being that I'm wrong."

"Me, too." I got up then. I could tell we were just about talked out. He slid off the desk and handed me my backpack.

"Don't assume the worst about yourself now, Katie."

"Thank you. And Mr. Grayson?"

"Yes."

"I'll see you in class tomorrow."

Day 8
Tuesday

I was almost late for school the next day. A nightmare had shaken me out of my hard-won sleep, something about a chainsaw-wielding person who turned out to be myself. I guessed the Jessica incident had a lot to do with it, plus my fear of being the villain in this note situation.

I shook my head to free it of the dream as I entered Oak Meadow.

That's when I saw the cluster of people down the hall, near the bulletin board.

Must be something interesting, I thought. Maybe Mrs. Perlman had finally had her baby.

There had been bets on whether my last year's algebra teacher would have a girl or a boy.

As I approached them, I heard a buzz of voices. Then a turquoise blur darted through the group: Rachel.

What was going on?

"This is total garbage!" she exclaimed. *It certainly wasn't baby news,* I thought, as I watched her snatch something off the board.

Hurriedly, I moved in closer, and that's when I felt, more than heard, the hush. As if in slow motion, everyone seemed to melt away, until just Rachel stood there, clutching something, as I drew even with her.

"What's going on?" I asked. "You don't want to know, Katie." Then it all came together.

"Oh, no! Let me see that." I reached out my hand, but she didn't give it to me right away.

"Look, I'm really sorry," she said. "I got it off the board as fast as I could."

"I know. I saw you. Thanks."

But the damage had been done. If it was what I thought it was, the leak was happening.

Don't let it be too explicit, I prayed.

"Here," Rachel said as she reluctantly handed it to me. From her expression, I guessed it was going to pack a punch.

What it did was to just about blow me away. I felt something roil in my stomach as my brain focused upon our names and one single word: lovers. But it was the photograph that made it worse than anything I could have imagined. If a picture is worth a thousand words, this one was downright damning.

"Oh, great! Rachel, how many people saw this?" I asked.

"I don't know. What are you going to do? How did someone get this photo of you and Grayson?"

"I have to warn him that this is out. It could be spreading around the school like wildfire even as we're talking."

"What can I do to help?"

"Just do what you did before, tell them it's garbage."

"But . . ."

"I can't explain right now, Rachel."

"Okay. See you later."

I didn't want to break this to Mr. Grayson, but it was better that he heard it from me than through the grapevine. Still, it was on rubber knees that I walked toward his office. I knew he dreaded a leak as much as I did.

He was just coming out the door when I got there, and his brows arched in surprise when he saw me. I could tell that he didn't know.

"Katie?"

"I need to talk to you," I said. "Something really awful has happened, and I don't think it should wait."

He glanced at his watch. Then he looked at me. He must have realized that it had to have been pretty important for me to be late for my first-period class.

"All right. Let me run down the hall and get my junior lit class broken into discussion groups. Go in and sit down. I'll be right back."

As I waited, I fell into a sort of stupor. I mean, this was going to go around! It seemed as unreal as my dream about brandishing a chainsaw. I was still floating on that sea of unreality when Mr. Grayson strode purposefully into the room.

"What's happening?" he asked.

"It's out."

His face turned as pale as a sheet. "Tell me."

"This was on the bulletin board near the trophy case," I said as I handed him the newest communique.

"On the bulletin board? I'm almost afraid to look." When he did, his expression changed to total disbelief. Then a deep rose color washed over his face.

"That's why I wanted to let you know right away."

"I'm glad you did. It's terrible! Where did the person get this picture of us?"

"It must have been when you were leaving my house."

"That's right. Your dog charged at my ankles and bowled you over in the process."

"And when I started to fall, you grabbed me."

"That's not how it looks, though," he said, shaking his head. I knew what he meant. It looked like one last embrace by the back door. It looked . . . intimate.

"Katie, how many people saw this?"

"Ten people—maybe twelve—were standing there when I walked into the building."

"But any number could have passed by before that. Oh, my," he said as he ran his fingers through his hair in the now-familiar gesture. "And you pulled it off the board? What did you say to the group?"

"No. Rachel Stamm was the one who took it off. She told everyone it was garbage. Since I hadn't seen the picture at that point, I didn't say anything. I still hadn't seen it when they just sort of drifted away when they saw me walk up."

"Good for her. Well, Katie, I don't know how I'm going to do it with this on my mind, but I do have classes to teach, including the one waiting for me now. I think you should attend all of yours, also. I'll give you a pass to get into first period. I don't think we should do a lot of explaining. Let's try, instead, to act as normal as possible and see how the wind blows.

"I'm going to have to share this now, though."

"I realize that. I'm sorry."

"I know. I am, too. This new development is serious." He thought for a few moments and went on with, "On the other hand, maybe it's not an entirely negative thing that this is coming to a head."

"How can you say that?" I asked in astonishment.

"I'm not trying to downplay the repercussions of this. It's just that the stress has been terrible for both of us. As difficult as it may be, let's try to keep calm and take this one step at a time."

I knew he was as freaked out as I was, but when he looked at me and said, "We're going to beat this, Katie. Remember that" I felt reassured.

"I'll try. Shall I come to class?"

"Of course."

That didn't mean it was easy. Whispers followed me, and probably Mr. Grayson, down the halls, and I felt eyes boring holes into me in my classes . . . people wondering, imagining, and maybe even believing this terrible thing.

I thought the hardest class would be his, but because we were together, armed with the truth, it actually wasn't as mortifying as I'd expected it to be.

In fact, it was in his class that, afraid for both him and myself, I felt another, worse kind of dread evaporate in a wave of elation.

I hadn't brought this on! Not only had the note already been on the bulletin board when I walked into the building, but there was no way I could have taken that picture of us. Why, I could cross my heart. I knew then that whatever else happened, I could live with myself without shame— and that was something.

As we turned in our persuasive letters, I even came outside myself and the situation long enough to wonder if Elena had read and thought about my original longhand version.

"I'll have these back promptly," Mr. Grayson told us. He was staying so together that I really admired him right then.

"Does he know?" Rachel asked as we left the room.

"Yeah. It really shook him."

"You'd never know it."

"He's a true professional," I said, which made me hope all the more that this wouldn't damage his reputation.

Then Rachel and I separated before third period.

Before I got there, I was caught up in the whispers around me in the hall, when a tap on my shoulder startled me. I spun around to face a bewildered Paul Dumont, who pulled me into a little alcove with him.

"What are you doing?" I asked.

"What's going on, Katie?"

"What do you mean?"

"I saw the picture."

"Oh."

"Is that all you can say?" he asked with amazement. "People are talking about it. My buddies . . ."

"What do you believe?" I interrupted, sick at heart. "I don't know what to think."

"There's nothing going on, Paul."

"If you say so." He shook his head. "That picture . . . Look, I've got to go."

He pivoted around without really looking at me, and my heart sank as I realized he was leaving.

"Paul," I called after him with a funny little squeak in my voice as tears welled, "It's not what you think." But I wasn't sure if he had heard me, and my eyes were still damp when I walked into geometry.

Did Paul believe this awful accusation? When I remembered our date and, especially, the duet and his gentle goodnight kiss, I felt totally sick. Was this going to break us up just when we were getting started?

Geometry was a blur as I fought back that fear. At lunch, there was a buzz that I sensed was about what had been on the bulletin board, and my nerves unraveled even more. Maren and Laura didn't help.

"Why didn't you tell us?" Maren asked. She seemed really put out that I hadn't.

"Oh, you heard."

"Yeah," she said.

"That picture was really hot. I was one of the ones standing around the board just before you came," Laura informed me.

Her news came as a surprise. It also made me wonder why, if she had been there, she hadn't waited around and said something, as Rachel had. What kind of friend was she?

"I didn't see you," was all I could say.

"Well?" she prodded.

"Well what?"

"Aren't you going to tell us more about it?" Maren asked.

What did they want, anyway? A blow-by-blow description of how stressed out Mr. Grayson and I were?

"There's nothing going on, Maren. Somebody's accusing us of something that's a total lie."

"But Grayson," Laura said almost dreamily, "is so . . ."

". . . sexy," Maren finished for her. And then they actually laughed. Did they think this situation was romantic or something? I couldn't believe it. First, Paul; now, them.

"Look," I said, "This hasn't been fun and games. It's been an ordeal. I just don't feel like talking about it now."

"You're being awfully defensive," Laura told me.

"Defensive?"

"Yeah," Maren agreed.

I could have told them what we were really doing when that picture had been taken, but even if I had felt free to discuss the situation, I realized that I just didn't want to share anything with Maren and Laura. Instinctively, I looked for Elena, but I didn't see her.

I did see someone else.

"Paul's coming this way," I said as my heart skipped a couple of beats. Was he really on his way over to talk to me? What did he want, anyway? To tell me the awful things his buddies were saying? All I knew for sure was that I didn't want those two listening in on a continuation of Paul's and my conversation in the alcove. "I'm going to talk to him."

Maren and Laura just nodded, and it was with mixed feelings that I got up before Paul reached our table.

"That didn't look like a very good conversation," he remarked, glancing in their direction. They were watching us.

"It wasn't."

"Let's forget them and find a place to sit down," he suggested. We found a couple of chairs at a table near the door. Sort of nervously he offered me some candy.

"Skittle?"

"Thanks." I ate one and sighed deeply. The ball was in his court.

"Is this picture thing what you told me about? You know, the harassment?"

"Mmm hmm. I never thought it would get this far, though. I mean, you know, out in the open. I'm so embarrassed! I'm also sorry that you had to see the picture of Mr. Grayson and me. It's not what it looks like."

"You don't have to explain."

"But I want to. I fell, and he was just breaking it. I don't have any idea who took that picture or why this is happening."

"Listen, Katie, I'm sorry about the way I acted earlier. I knew it had to be something like that, but my buddies were really razzing me, and you'll have to admit that the way he was holding you looks like what people are talking about."

"Yeah, I know. It's just that it's not."

"I believe you, and I want you to know that you have my support."

"It really means a lot to me, Paul. Thanks."

"I'm not trying to make light of this, but if you feel like trying to get your mind off of it, there's a Jane Austen movie on downtown. Do you want to go this weekend?"

I couldn't believe he was actually asking me out again with this breaking loose. It was like a breath of fresh air wafting through the stench. More, it was a vote of confidence just when I needed one.

"I'd like that," I said. Our eyes met, and something special flickered between us. "Okay. We'll work out the details later. Katie, Ms. Daniels just walked in. I think she may be coming over this way. I'll make myself scarce if she does."

"Okay."

Tanisha Daniels was a large woman with a rather commanding presence, but there was nothing standoffish about her. In fact, she often stopped by the cafeteria to chat with students, just because she liked people, I thought, and it would be no big deal if she sat down with me.

Paul was right. She had been heading our way.

"May I?" the school counselor asked as she pointed to an empty chair at our table.

"Sure."

"Hi, Ms. Daniels" Paul greeted. "I was just leaving. I'll talk to you later, Katie."

I smiled as he left.

"He's a perceptive young man," Ms. Daniels remarked as she waved him off

"I know."

"Katie, I heard about your situation. Is there anything I can do?"

"Thank you. I don't know. This whole thing's just gotten way out of hand."

"I talked to Mr. Grayson," she said.

"Oh, I'm glad."

"He's worried about you. Katie, he told me you can't imagine who is doing this, or why. It must be very stressful."

"You can say that again, but I guess I'm doing okay. Ms.

Daniels, why do people do things like this? Is this person crazy?"

"I'm not comfortable with that word. Emotionally disturbed is probably a better description, although even that term covers a wide range of behavior. Keep in mind, also, that so-called normal people sometimes do strange things.

"As for the why of it, I wish I had a pat answer for you, but something like this is complex. Generally speaking, though, the kind of person who does this is probably going through some kind of trauma and is acting it out. Behavior like this can also follow a pattern."

"A pattern?"

"Yes, the person doing this may have done something similar in the past. And that's where I may be of help."

When she paused, I asked, "What do you mean?"

"I thought that maybe I'd do a little detective work and see what I can come up with. Since I have access to student records, I can do some scanning. I may run across a red flag or two. Mr. Grayson has already mentioned some names as a starting point."

"Wow! That sounds like a good plan."

"Tim thinks so, too. Anyway, if you need someone to talk to, I'm here. I would also like to give you my home phone number," she added as she jotted it onto a slip of paper. "Don't hesitate to call."

"I really appreciate this"

She got up to leave as I took the piece of paper.

"We'll get to the bottom of this, Katie," she said so emphatically that for the first time in many days, I felt that we actually would.

I had no way of knowing that I was on the very brink of finding out.

"**D**ecahedra!" I said in exasperation.

"What was that?" Mrs. Pemberton was at the kitchen sink, where she was just finishing the dinner dishes. It was her bridge night, so we'd eaten early.

"Ten-sided solid figures," I explained from a table in the adjoining family room. "I wish Eric were here. He'd have this done in a snap." Eric was my genius brother who was in grad school back East. Mrs. Pemberton walked closer.

"What is it you have to do?"

"I'm making a three-dimensional figure for geometry. Shape lab, my teacher calls it. The tricky part is getting the poster-board sides exactly even." I'd already squashed three lopsided attempts and was about half-finished with my fourth.

"It's time for me to leave for Marge's. You'll be all right now, won't you? As I said before, giving up bridge wouldn't be the end of the world."

Over dinner, I'd finally told her about the harassment,

downplaying it a lot, and even though she didn't know many details, having her support felt good. At this point, it didn't matter a whole lot, either, if she shared it with her bridge club.

"Oh, no, please go. I'll be fine . . . fine, that is, if I can get this stupid shape made," I laughed.

"Well, be careful with that scissors. It's a wicked-looking pair."

"I will," I promised. Then she was on her way.

The house did feel kind of empty without her. It had been such a weird day, from the picture on the bulletin board, through telling Mr. Grayson, to enduring all the whispers and stares. Although I kept expecting Mrs. Hovis, the principal, to call me down to her office, that never happened. She was out for a conference, someone had said.

There had been support from people like Ms. Daniels, Rachel, and Paul. My heart had also been warmed when people I hardly knew had put in a kind word.

Still, there had been the sort of morbid curiosity and speculation that didn't help me at all. I'd felt so totally on-stage all day that it had been draining.

I turned what energy I had left back to the decahedron. I'm not sure how long it took me to finish the thing—it actually looked pretty good—but I had just set it down when the doorbell rang.

Cognac, at my feet, hadn't even heard it. She was getting so old.

I was on my way to answer the door when I stopped. "Emotionally disturbed" Ms. Daniels had called the note sender. *Better not answer it,* I thought. Still, sending notes was a far cry from brandishing a weapon or doing anything violent, and I did want to confront whoever was doing this and put a stop to it.

It was probably just Rachel, anyway, or Paul, I decided,

as my heart turned over. To be on the safe side, I peeked through the peephole. Then I swung back the door.

"Elena!"

"Hi. Can I come in?" When her eyes didn't meet mine, I felt the strain of our messed-up friendship full force. Even so, the fact that she was here, at my house after all this time, had to mean something.

The letter; she must have read my letter.

"Well, sure. Um, do you want a soda or something?" I asked as she stepped over the threshold.

"Not right now, but thanks. Katie, could we talk?"

"Yeah, but let's get out of the entryway." I laughed nervously. Then I led her toward the family room.

As we walked in and Cognac rolled over in delight at the very sight of her, memories kaleidoscoped, the two of us cutting out paper dolls on the floor, making arts and crafts projects as Brownies, and singing carols with my parents and brothers as we sipped hot chocolate. I motioned to the couch where Elena and I had giggled nonstop together and shared zillions of secrets. Could we somehow get it right again?

I thought so when she automatically took her side of the couch, but when she looked down at her hands self-consciously and couldn't seem to get any words out, I realized more than ever that this was now and those memories were then. If we'd had some kind of argument, I think maybe I'd have known what to say to her, but we hadn't argued. I just didn't know for sure what was going on with her and had to let the first words be hers. When they came, they shot out in an explosive little sentence.

"Oh, Katie, can you ever forgive me?"

"Forgive you?"

"I've been such a flake."

"Well . . ."

"No, let me say what I need to, and you can decide if you still want to be my friend." When I nodded, she went on with, "I've just never been so shaken up in my whole life. I mean, we were a family, and it just all crumbled to dust. Dad was suddenly gone with Tyler, and Mom went into herself. She doesn't believe in divorce, you know, and I'd hear her moaning and crying all night. I might as well have lost both parents.

"I hated Dad for leaving, and I started hating her for making me feel like her mother or something. I was the one who had to make sure we got fed—stuff like that. It just got so complicated. It got so . . . consuming. I just pushed everyone away.

"But, Katie, I don't know how I could have done it to you. I never meant to hurt you. I'm a terrible friend! I'm so ashamed!" she finished with a sob as her head sank into her hands.

What could I do to help her? She was so shaken up and guilt-ridden.

"Elena," I finally said, but she didn't look up. "Kiddie," I amended, using that long-ago nickname. That brought her head up, and when her tear-stained eyes met mine, I started crying along with her. We hugged like Velcro bunnies for the longest time, and as we finally pulled apart, I said, "Of course I still want to be your friend."

"Thank heavens!"

"I know you've been going through an ordeal. My heart's ached for you, you know."

"I know. I started getting my act back together when I realized that whatever happens with Mom and Dad, I'm me. I'm Elena Rose Banning, and I have choices here. Maybe I can't make Mom and Dad stay together or bring Tyler back or make my mom smile, but I can take charge of my own life, Katie. I can sink or swim. I can let this make me bitter or better."

"Right on!"

"And it's weird what helped me snap out of my funk."

"What did?" I asked.

"Believe it or not, this bizarre situation you're in."

"You read my letter."

"I did, and I heard the stuff at school today. It must creep you out."

"You said it! But how did that help you?"

"It's made me feel for you, Katie, made me get outside myself and my own family's problems a little."

"I'm glad," I said, "that it's had at least one positive effect, because it's gotten really weird."

"Tell me about it." I knew she was asking as a true friend, not an idle curiosity-seeker, and I described the notes and talking to Mr. Grayson and Ms. Daniels.

"I'm worried about his reputation here, Elena. He's so new to teaching, and if anyone ever believed this stuff, it could ruin things for him."

"That's like you, to be concerned for him. Listen, your good reputations count for something. Of course . . ."

"What were you going to say?"

"Just that there are people like Sharon Fleming."

Sharon Fleming? She was the one Mr. Grayson had suspended from tennis, the one I'd beaten out for choir. Sharon Fleming was one of our prime suspects.

"What about her?" I asked.

"Oh, she's encouraging people to believe there's something going on between you and Mr. Grayson."

"Well, it's not true!"

"You don't have to convince me. Um, Katie, how well do you know Rachel Stamm?"

Oh, great! I thought, Elena and I were making progress. Was she going to come down on my new friend now?

Was she jealous of our friendship?

"Rachel?" I asked.

"Yeah. What do you really know about her?"

"She's nice and easy-to-like."

"And she knows about these notes?"

"Well, yeah. Some of them, anyway."

"Did you know she used to live in California?"

"Seattle," I corrected. "Rachel's from Seattle."

"Katie . . ."

"So? What are you getting at?" I interrupted. Elena was wrong, and I didn't want to fight with her about something so unimportant, but I didn't like the way she was implying that Rachel was a liar, either.

"Well, it's going to sound like I'm trying to trash her, so here, take a look at this."

Elena handed me what looked like a copy of a school picture.

"What's this?" I asked.

"A FAX. She's younger, but it's Rachel, isn't it?"

"Yeah, I guess it is. She was pretty even with braces. Where did you get this picture?"

I don't know if you knew my dad and Tyler are living in Sherman Oaks. That's in the San Fernando Valley."

"Laura said something about it. That's right by L.A., isn't it? But what does that have to do with this picture of Rachel?"

"I'm getting to that. Now, this is going to sound really strange, but the girl in the picture—Rachel—is the same girl who used to go to Tyler's new school."

"I don't know where you're coming from. Why would I think you are trashing Rachel just because of the small-world coincidence that Tyler ended up at her old school?"

"There's a lot more to it," Elena said so sympathetically that it scared me.

"I'm listening."

"I'm having trouble telling you about this because I know Rachel is your friend."

"Trouble? Well, just spit it out."

Elena took a deep breath. "I think she's behind the notes."

"Oh, come on! Rachel has been nothing but supportive throughout this whole thing."

"Just listen to me. Katie, Tyler and I were talking on the phone, and I mentioned that somebody's been harassing you. We just got to talking about that kind of thing. You know, tormenting others, stalking—the whole range of it—and he mentioned this beautiful, red-haired weirdo who had been at his school the previous year."

"Oh, and you think this weirdo was Rachel? Just tell me why you think she's mixed up in this."

"The girl in this picture," Elena said, pointing to the FAX sheet, "harassed her friend in California with notes and stuff. It all led to a terrible tragedy when the other girl fell down a flight of stairs. Katie, Tyler said that Rachel deliberately pushed her."

"Pushed her? Rachel? I've never heard anything so preposterous." But that didn't keep me from asking, "What happened to the girl?"

"She died."

"Died?"

Elena nodded. That poor girl! But even though it was a tragedy no matter how you looked at it, I just couldn't picture Rachel Stamm being violent. I knew from experience what it was like to be falsely accused, and I knew from what Mr. Grayson had told me about his experience in Ohio that people do go on unfounded witch hunts.

"I feel awful for the girl," I said, "but if there's one thing I've learned, especially lately, it's that rumors can be cruel and totally without substance. There has to be some mistake. It can't be Rachel who pushed that girl or who's doing this to me now."

"I understand how you feel, but what if it is Rachel? It sounded like a lot more than rumor to me, and the Stamms did move away shortly after Lisa died. Besides, there's more."

"Go ahead."

"Tyler did some nosing around at my insistence, and he found out that Rachel supposedly left another old school for medical reasons. I don't know if that was connected with violence or harassment, but something's not right. Katie, I'm afraid for you now."

Elena had always had these odd, on-target instincts, so it was impossible not to respect her fear for me now. Were the things she was telling me about Rachel and the red flags that Ms. Daniels had meant? Could it be Rachel, after all?

"I don't know what to believe," I said.

"Look, you're not convinced. That's okay, but will you promise me something?"

"If I can."

"Just be careful. Katie, I hope it's not Rachel."

"You do?"

"Yeah, because I'm your friend."

My mind was simply boggling, but Elena was absolutely right about one thing. "You are, Elena, and I'll think about everything you've said."

"Good. Now, as much as I hate to say it, I've got to get back home. We haven't had dinner yet. Who knows, maybe this will be the night I can draw Mom out a little more."

"I hope so," I said, remembering that Elena had a set of her own problems.

She gave Cognac's belly a good rub on her way out, and I knew things were back on track with us when she left, not by the front, as she had entered, but by the back door she had used five hundred times in the past. She paused for a moment at the door.

"Katie, maybe you'd better no. . . No, I'm not going to say it. I'll be home. Call me if you need to talk. And be careful."

"I will. Thanks."

As I walked back through the family room, I picked up the FAX. My heart rate speeded up as I looked again at the picture. It was Rachel or a dead ringer. But Rachel sending notes? Worse, Rachel pushing a girl to her death? I shook my head in denial.

For one thing, she had no motive for zeroing in on me. We'd gotten along fine from day one, and hadn't she proven her friendship by not assuming the worst when I'd told her about my seizure disorder or shared this ongoing note situation with her? She'd even been the one to pull this morning's note off the bulletin board to protect me.

What's more, she had everything going for her: great looks, good grades, nice house. She had friends, and the guy she was interested in had asked her out. Hardly the portrait of a crazy person.

No, not crazy, I corrected even as I thought it. But whatever the right term, what did I know about really troubled people? Were they always easy to spot, or were some of them masters at hiding their inner turmoil? Red flags: maybe they were sometimes subtle.

I thought again about Elena's uncannily accurate instinct. Then I reached into my jeans pocket and pulled out Tanisha Daniels' small memo sheet. Should I call her? Would I be ratting out Rachel? Still, if it did happen to be Rachel, wouldn't I be helping her, as well as protecting myself, if I shared what Elena had told me?

It was that belief that led me to dial her home number.

I listened to her phone ringing. Then I sighed in relief

as she answered.

"Hello, this is Tanisha. We're not able to come to the phone right now, but . . . ." I filtered out the rest of the recorded message. What had I been about to say, anyway? How do you tell someone that you have doubts about your friend?

Beep!

"Hi, Ms. Daniels. It's Katie Krieg calling at 8:05 Tuesday. I've learned some things since we talked at lunchtime. I think you might want to check out . . ."

Click.

What was that? I stopped talking in mid-sentence at the unexpected sound. Was the phone dead or something?

"Hello?" Of course no one said anything. Ms. Daniels hadn't even been on the line. I put the receiver back into its cradle and picked up the phone again.

There was no dial tone. Amazed, I held the receiver fast to my ear and tapped the button, thinking I could somehow revive the instrument, but nothing happened. It was as dead as a doornail.

As I hung up, the most incredible foreboding oozed through me. I was home alone with no contact with the outside world. I could open the door and run out into the night, but was someone lying in wait out there? Had someone cut our phone line?

Or was I just being melodramatic? Notes: they were only notes. Upsetting notes, that's true, but, still, they were just pieces of paper. Why, you couldn't even call the police for something like that, when no threats had been made. So, I was being silly, wasn't I? Phones did suddenly go out. I'd walk across the street and report the outage on the neighbor's phone.

First, though, I had to go to the bathroom, or I'd burst. It was when I came out that she was standing there.

"**Y**ou startled me!" I exclaimed. "What are you doing here?"

"Taking care of something," Rachel said. She seemed like she always did, and I tried to relax. "I knocked, but I guess you didn't hear me."

"I guess not. I was in the powder room."

"I hope you don't mind my just walking in. The back door was unlocked."

Hadn't I locked it behind Elena? I wasn't sure.

"No, that's okay," I said.

"I have something for you to read that you might find . . . um . . . illuminating."

I felt uneasy standing in the shadowy hallway. "Let's go into the family room and sit down," I suggested.

"It's about the note business."

Did the fact that Rachel wanted to show me something mean it wasn't her, after all? My hope didn't exactly soar, but the benefit of the doubt remained open, and I was glad right then that I hadn't had the chance to say Rachel's name to Ms. Daniels on the phone.

"You can't know how badly I want to get to the bottom of this," I said.

"I'll bet."

"Sit down and show me what you've got."

"Mind if we have a soda or something?" she asked, still standing. Actually, I didn't want to take the time to get anything, but I couldn't very well refuse, either.

"Sure." While I took a couple of cans and some ice out of the fridge, she looked around.

"What's this?" she called as she lifted my decahedron off the table.

"My masterpiece." I explained the project as I brought our drinks.

"Thanks," Rachel said as I handed her a glass and a can. I set mine down, unpoured. Then we sat down.

"Well, let me see it. The suspense is killing me."

Rachel laughed. "Before I do, I just want you to know that Mr. Grayson knows."

"Oh, you showed it to him?"

"Yeah, it'll probably freaked him out even more than the pictures did."

Why would she show anything to Mr. Grayson? The more I thought about it, the stranger it seemed.

"Does he know who the note sender is now?" I asked. Then it hit me. Pictures, plural! Had I heard her right? Had Rachel added an "s" to the word? No one but Mr. Grayson, the note sender, and I knew there had been more than one picture. This was a definite red flag, but was it proof that Rachel was my tormentor?

I didn't know what to do. I could ask her to leave or demand an explanation, but if she were the one, that could be exactly the wrong approach. On the other hand, would it be a mistake to act like nothing was wrong? Would she see through me and take it out on me? How did a person deal with someone who was that troubled, if, indeed, she was?

"Probably by now he knows," Rachel said, cutting into my mental debate. Then some words popped out of my mouth that I immediately regretted.

"Do you know?"

Something in her amber stare made my skin crawl. What if she were dangerous?

What if she had even pushed that girl in California? As much as I wanted to see the paper she'd alluded to, I suddenly needed to get out of the house, with its dead phone—out where there were other people. Mrs. Pemberton wouldn't be back for at least two hours, and I couldn't count on anyone else showing up.

Rachel still hadn't answered my question.

"Say," I suggested, "why don't you bring whatever it is you have to show me, and we can get some dessert at that new coffee house."

"Oh, I'm not very hungry. You can just look at it right here. I'll drink my soda while you read it."

"All right." Just reading something couldn't be dangerous. Besides, maybe I was just spooked. Maybe whatever she had for me to read would exonerate her. It had to, didn't it? It couldn't be my friend who had done this. Then why are you feeling so uneasy, Katie Krieg? I asked myself

As Rachel opened her bag, I poured myself some soda in an attempt to stem my doubts.

"Here," she said, handing me a computer printout.

"What's this?" It looked like a letter, and the salutation had my name on it: "'Dear Katie . . . .'" I flipped to the last page for a signature, but there was none.

"Just read it," she said quietly as she picked up her glass.

Dear Katie,

It's funny how the little things in life can be so enormous. Things like a locket. Do you know that if you hadn't happened to be wearing a round one of a certain kind, none of this would be happening? That's what I mean about the irony of the little things.

"What? My locket?" I said as my hand stroked the piece of jewelry on its chain around my neck. What was this person—Rachel?—getting at?

"It's self-explanatory," she told me. "Read on."

You see, I have one very much like yours, only I wear mine in fear, shame, and anger. The anger is so great, in fact, that when I see someone else wearing one, something in me sometimes snaps.

It all goes back to when I was eleven. My father came into my room one night and gave me a little velvet box. Inside, was the locket so much like yours. Only, of course, mine had my name engraved on the back.

"Put it on," he told me, and I did. "You will be my special princess whenever you wear this."

That's when he began doing unspeakable things to me. Always, I had to put the locket on, and always he warned me not to tell. But I finally did tell my mother about the abuse, and when she didn't believe me, it was like a dagger in my heart. She just sent me to a psychologist "to help me with my horrible 'story," and he said I was acting out my pubescent fantasies! I got angry.

I got enraged!

I could see in the mirror that I was getting
pretty, and I hated my prettiness. Even
more, I hated girls my age who wore round
lockets and looked like girls-next-door. I
wanted to be them, not me.

When I couldn't be them, I wanted them to
be humiliated, scarred, ruined. So I found
a way to penetrate their perfect little lives
with worry, fear, maybe even scandal.

And it worked, except for Lisa.

Oh my God! It was Rachel! In had had any lingering
doubts, the mention of the girl who had died settled it for
good. The realization sent a current of something so awful
sizzling through me that I had to struggle just to catch my
breath.

What should I do? Almost involuntarily, I looked at
Rachel. She looked so calm, just sitting there sipping her
drink. Maybe I needed to know what else she had written
before I even thought about how to deal with her. I read on.

Lisa guessed it was me sending the notes
about her and our biology teacher. She
had the nerve to call me crazy! We were
standing at the top of the stairs, and just
then the sunlight came through the landing
window and shone on her locket like a
spotlight. I hated her more than ever at that
moment. I had to do something.

So, I pushed her.

I still have to wear the locket sometimes.
I want to run as far from him as I can, but
he says he will find me if I try to. He said
there's no escape, and I believe him.

So, what else can I do? We move every

time I get into trouble, and every time, I just find a new victim.

This time it was you, Katie Krieg.

As I finished reading the letter, suddenly I knew full-force what people mean when they warn you to be careful what you wish for. I now knew who and why, but what was I going to do with that knowledge?

Even though I was still looking at the printout, Rachel must have guessed that I'd read the whole thing.

"What do you think of it?" There was something weird in her voice, almost as if she expected me to praise her composition.

"It's really sad," I said as calmly as I could. "Did you say that Mr. Grayson has read it?"

"Yeah, he probably has by now. He has a copy."

Would he know it was Rachel, though? Elena had just told me about Lisa, so that name wouldn't ring any bells for him, as it had for me. I had to hope he'd figure it out.

And then there was Ms. Daniels. Maybe she would come home, get my aborted call, and realize something was up.

I had to keep Rachel talking. I had to keep her calm. And, most of all, I couldn't call her crazy.

Suddenly, though, the instinct to get away from her was overpowering. How did you talk to someone like her? How did you keep her calm? I got up.

"Sit down. Where were you going?" she spat.

"I forgot about my soda," I ad-libbed with a sinking feeling. "Would you like another?"

"No, thanks."

I poured some of mine into my glass, spilling a little.

"You're trembling," she observed.

"That letter is heartbreaking."

"Oh?"

"Yeah, I mean abused by her own father. And then not to have anyone believe her or help her."

"Maybe she deserved it."

"Oh, Rachel, nobody deserves that. Those are parents we're talking about, and parents have the responsibility to nurture and protect at all times."

She looked me up and down. "You know," she pronounced.

"I know?"

"That it's me."

"Rachel, I believe you. Mr. Grayson will, too, when he reads this. Let us get you some help."

"Help! Help?" The word seemed to have lit a fuse. I wanted to get back up and run, but at the same time, I felt bolted to the couch.

"Yeah," was all I could say.

"It's too late for that. I'm totally ruined."

"No, you're not. It's never too . . ."

"Don't you tell me what I am or am not, Katie Krieg!" She sprang off the couch and started pacing the room.

"I'm sorry."

Could I make it to the back door and get away from her? It wasn't far, but Rachel was a lot taller than I, with long legs meant for running. With a sick feeling, I doubted it.

It was as though she read my thoughts.

"Don't even think about it," she warned. "We're not through here."

"Okay." She was so agitated that I obeyed. *Keep her talking,* I reminded myself.

"Don't you wonder how I got that photo of you and Grayson?"

"Yeah."

"I didn't go to the mall on Saturday. There was something in your voice on the phone. I felt like you were putting me off, hiding something from me, so I came over to talk to you. Well, I saw him going into your house. I ran home and got my camera, and well, I just waited until he came out. Boy, did I get a bonus!"

"What do you mean?"

"You two really do have something going."

"That's not true. Didn't you see the dog trip me? Mr. Grayson was just trying to keep me from falling down the stairs."

"Oh, I saw that, all right. But he held you longer than he had to, Katie, and you—both of you—enjoyed it. I know about these things. I could tell."

"It's in your imagination," I said.

That set her off again.

"How dare you!"

She started playing with the scissors, and when she didn't put them down, I started thinking of poor Lisa on the stairs. Sick with dread, I reached up and unfastened my locket.

"What are you doing?" she demanded.

"I thought I'd take this off. It seems cruel to remind you of your ordeal."

"Leave it on!"

"But why?"

"I want to remember. I want to despise you. I want to finish this thing!"

"Finish . . ."

The rest of the sentence died in my throat as she lifted the scissors and held them, threateningly, pointed end toward me.

She was going to kill me! Until that moment, a part of

me had thought she wouldn't get violent with me.

Think, Katie . . .

She was between me and the back door, so that was out. Light glinted on the scissors as if to tell me how foolish trying to get past her would be.

Front door, my brain commanded.

Then I was running. In a nightmare, I felt my legs pumping for life, felt myself seeming to only inch toward the door . . . and freedom.

Run . . . run . . . .

As I turned the comer into the foyer, I saw Rachel out of one eye. Crazed, scissors in hand, she was gaining on me, ready to lunge.

Faster, I ordered.

She was coming so quickly, though, that I knew it was just a matter of time—extremely little time. What could I do?

That's when it all happened. I sidestepped to avoid her just as Cognac charged at her like a miniature orange bull.

Rachel tripped, and the lethal blades slashed through the air inches from my face. Just then, the door burst open.

"Katie!" a female voice cried.

"Are you all right?" a male voice called. It was Ms. Daniels and Mr. Grayson. "She tried to kill me," I said in disbelief.

Rachel was on the foyer floor, unhurt, but she still had the scissors. "Let me have those," Ms. Daniels coaxed.

"No."

I heard Ms. Daniels whisper something to Mr. Grayson about her cellular phone and 911. Moments passed, and I was vaguely aware of him giving my address.

Then I sucked in my breath. Rachel had the long, deadly scissors pointed at her chest, right over her heart.

"Don't do that, Rachel!" Mr. Grayson called as he got off the phone.

"Give me a good reason not to."

"People care," Ms. Daniels said.

"Katie hates me!"

"No, I don't, Rachel."

"Then prove it," she defied.

"How?"

"Come over and sit by me."

Sit by her? Did she think I was out of my mind? Even with two other people there, she could stab me in an instant. Wasn't that what she had wanted all along? Hadn't she written that she wanted her victims to be humiliated, scarred, ruined?

"Rachel?" Ms. Daniels said.

"Shut up!" Rachel commanded as she positioned the scissors even closer to her body.

She was going to do it if someone didn't show her the compassion she needed just then, and for some reason, I was the one she was counting on.

"I'm coming," I said.

"No, Katie!" cried Mr. Grayson.

I moved toward Rachel. Totally focused upon her and the scissors, I sat down beside her, wondering if it would be the biggest—the last—mistake of my life. And even if she didn't hurt me, was I stupid to think she wouldn't kill herself right in front of me?

"Rachel," I said softly.

And then a strange thing happened. Instead of answering, she slowly turned the weapon away from herself, put it down, and began humming. As she sat and hummed, she rocked back and forth.

Mr. Grayson walked up to us, kicked the scissors away, and made sure that I was all right. Then he asked, "What's that melody?"

"It's from *The Sleeping Beauty Ballet*," Ms. Daniels

informed us as she sat down beside Rachel.

I got up and started bawling then, for Rachel, and Mr. Grayson put an arm around my shoulders.

"The princess," I said softly through my tears.

"Her father's name for her," he remarked, shaking his head sadly. Rachel just kept humming and rocking as Ms. Daniels sat beside her.

She didn't even seem to know it when the police arrived and took her away. Like the fairytale princess, she was out of it.

One Month Later

As a golden alder leaf fluttered close to my face on its way to the ground, Mr. Grayson said, "'Colorful ghosts of summer.' That's how one of my students described the falling leaves."

We were leaving Oak Meadow at the same time by pure chance, since I had stayed after choir practice to get a solo just right for the choral director.

"That's a good description."

He gestured to an old-fashioned iron bench. "Let's sit down for a minute."

"Okay."

"How are you doing, Katie? I see you in class five times a week, but how are you really doing?"

I saw from the way he looked at me that he really cared, and maybe this was the epilogue—the something unfinished the psychologist had mentioned—that Mr. Grayson and I needed.

"I'm hanging in. At first, I had recurrent nightmares and feelings of betrayal. I was . . . I don't know . . . haunted by the feeling that I should have known all along that it was Rachel. I felt like such a fool, Mr. Grayson. A psychologist has helped me put it into perspective, though." My parents, Elena, and Paul were also helping a lot by being so supportive.

"I'm glad to hear that."

"How are you doing?"

"I'm hanging in there, too."

"Good," I said. I was going to ask him if he had heard anything about Rachel, but he spoke again before I could.

"There's something else I want to talk to you about. It's about the picture."

"Which one?"

"The photograph of us."

"Oh."

He fidgeted on the bench as he seemed to search for the right words.

"I reached out for you automatically when you started to fall, but the picture captured an unguarded moment, Katie, when I was not acting as a teacher."

"I know."

"I thought maybe you did."

I just nodded.

"At first," he said, "I castigated myself for having held you too long."

"You don't have to explain."

He shook his head. "I think we need some closure on this."

Hadn't I thought about that moment and all of this, too? "Me, too."

"We were victims with raw emotions. I'm sorry, though, if I've made you uncomfortable around me."

"Don't worry. I'm uncomfortable with what Rachel did, but I'm not uncomfortable around you. I'm . . . oh . . . I can't think of the right word."

"Aware?" he supplied.

That was it. I was aware of him as I wasn't aware of my other teachers, or even as I had been of him when this began. But I didn't know how to explain it to him. It wasn't really a romantic thing. Or was it? Whatever it was, we'd been involved in an incredibly bizarre, emotional situation, and I felt something.

When I looked into his ocean-colored eyes, I felt a current of understanding pass between us.

"Yes," I confirmed. "Aware."

"How could we not be, Katie? People change all the time. This has changed us, and we can't go back to the simpler feelings we had before."

"And this being aware is part of that change."

"That's right," he agreed.

When I looked at him and realized how easily I could drown in the depths of those caring eyes, I forced myself to change the subject.

"I just wish Rachel didn't have to suffer so. Have you heard anything about her lately? I've been so worried about her."

"That sounds like you," he said with a smile. "I'm sure she's going through a very painful, difficult time, but she is getting intensive therapy and the kind of support she's needed for years, Katie, and that's a huge breakthrough in itself Now that her father has been exposed and the abuse is over, we can hope that in time she can rebuild her life. Your compassion was the start."

"Anybody would have done what I did."

"Don't sell yourself short. No, they wouldn't. What you did took courage."

"I had to do it. I just knew she was going to stab herself if I didn't stop her." I shook my head at the memory.

Just then, Mr. Grayson picked a bright orange

leaf off the bench and held it up so that the sunlight filtered through, highlighting its veins.

"See this leaf?" he asked. "It came from that maple tree that's changing even as we speak. In the spring, long after this leaf is compost, the tree will metamorphose with its delicate chartreuse halo."

"A rebirth," I nodded.

"Yes. Human beings, of course, are more complex than trees—and there are no guarantees—but we can hope that Rachel will experience a rebirth, also."

Then he handed me the leaf.

The End

About the Author

Virginia M. Scott loved to write novels and poetry and corresponded with her friends around the world, long before email.

Virginia was born in San Francisco, CA. in 1945. Her adoptive parents, Dr. and Mrs. Charles Muhleman, returned to La Porte, Indiana when she was an infant.

At the age of fourteen Virginia contracted meningitis and encephalitis causing the loss of hearing, serious balance problems, and epilepsy. In spite of her disabilities, she graduated from La Porte High School, received a BA degree with honors in English from Purdue North Central University, and completed a MA degree in Librarianship from the University of Washington. While at Purdue, Virginia won several writing contest and had her short stories published in *Portals*, a publication that included the winning stories.

In 1977 she married Dr. H. William Brelje, professor emeritus at Lewis and Clark College in Portland, Oregon.

They lived in Lake Oswego, Oregon from 1977 until her death in 2001. Virginia used their trips to Europe and Egypt to gather information for her writing. She especially enjoyed France and the French language and visited there on many occasions. Her favorite trip was to Egypt in 1990.

She assisted her husband in the creation of *A History of the Washington School for the Deaf*, and helped him develop his book, *Global Perspectives on the Education of the Deaf in Select Countries* in 1999.

Virginia is survived by her husband Bill, a daughter, Amy, who lives in Encino, California and three grandchildren.

Her Young Adult novels dealing with overcoming the challenges of hearing loss include: *The Palace of the Princes* (1978), *Belonging* (1986), *Balancing Act* (1997) and *Finding Abby* (2000).

The Carnelian Door and *Don't Cross Your Heart, Katie Krieg,* were published posthumously in 2017 by her husband, H. William Brelje.

(Endnotes)

1   *Getting to Know You*, Copyright 1951 by Richard Rodgers and
      Oscar Hammerstein II. Copyright renewed by Williamson Music